Oliver Goldsmith

The Poetical and Dramatic Works of Oliver Goldsmith, M.B.

Now first collected with an account of the life and writings of the author. Vol. 2

Oliver Goldsmith

The Poetical and Dramatic Works of Oliver Goldsmith, M.B.
Now first collected with an account of the life and writings of the author. Vol. 2

ISBN/EAN: 9783337094720

Printed in Europe, USA, Canada, Australia, Japan

THE
POETICAL
AND
DRAMATIC WORKS
OF
OLIVER GOLDSMITH, M. B.

NOW FIRST COLLECTED.

WITH AN ACCOUNT OF THE LIFE AND WRITINGS OF THE AUTHOR.

IN TWO VOLUMES.

LONDON:
PRINTED BY H. GOLDNEY,
FOR MESSIEURS RIVINGTON, T. CARNAN AND F. NEWBERY, IN ST. PAUL'S CHURCH-YARD; T. LOWNDES AND G. KEARSLEY, IN FLEET-STREET; T. CADELL AND T. EVANS IN THE STRAND.
MDCCLXXX.

PLAYS,

BY

DR. GOLDSMITH.

THE

GOOD-NATUR'D MAN:

A

COMEDY.

AS PERFORMED AT THE

THEATRE-ROYAL,

IN

COVENT-GARDEN.

FIRST PRINTED IN MDCCLXVIII.

PREFACE.

WHEN I undertook to write a comedy, I confess I was strongly prepossessed in favour of the poets of the last age, and strove to imitate them. The term, genteel comedy, was then unknown amongst us, and little more was desired by an audience, than nature and humour, in whatever walks of life they were most conspicuous. The author of the following scenes never imagined that more would be expected of him, and therefore to delineate character has been his principal aim. Those who know any thing of composition, are sensible, that in pursuing humour, it will sometimes lead us into the recesses of the mean; I was even tempted to look for it in the master of a spunging-house: but in deference to the public taste, grown of late, perhaps, too delicate, the scene of the bailiffs was retrenched in the representation. In deference also to the judgment of a few friends, who think in a particular way, the scene is here restored. The author submits it to the reader

reader in his closet; and hopes that too much refinement will not banish humour and character from ours, as it has already done from the French theatre. Indeed the French comedy is now become so very elevated and sentimental, that it has not only banished humour and Moliere from the stage, but it has banished all spectators too.

Upon the whole, the author returns his thanks to the public for the favourable reception which the Good-Natur'd Man has met with: and to Mr. Colman in particular, for his kindness to it. It may not also be improper to assure any, who shall hereafter write for the theatre, that merit, or supposed merit, will ever be a sufficient passport to his protection.

PROLOGUE,

WRITTEN BY

DR. JOHNSON:

SPOKEN BY

MR. BENSLEY.

PREST by the load of life, the weary mind
Surveys the general toil of human kind;
With cool submission joins the lab'ring train,
And social sorrow, loses half its pain:
Our anxious bard, without complaint, may share
This bustling season's epidemic care.
Like Cæsar's pilot, dignify'd by fate,
Tost in one common storm with all the great;
Distrest alike, the statesman and the wit,
When one a borough courts, and one the pit.
The busy candidates for power and fame,
Have hopes, and fears, and wishes, just the same;
Disabled both to combat, or to fly,
Must hear all taunts, and hear without reply.
Uncheck'd on both, loud rabbles vent their rage,
As mongrels bay the lion in a cage.
Th' offended burgess hoards his angry tale,
For that blest year when all that vote may rail;
Their schemes of spite the poet's foes dismiss,
Till that glad night, when all that hate may hiss.

" This day the powder'd curls and golden coat,"
Says ſwelling Criſpin, " begg'd a cobler's vote."
" This night, our wit," the pert apprentice cries,
" Lies at my feet, I hiſs him, and he dies."
The great, 'tis true, can charm th' electing tribe;
The bard may ſupplicate, but cannot bribe.
Yet judg'd by thoſe, whoſe voices ne'er were ſold,
He feels no want of ill-perſuading gold;
But confident of praiſe, if praiſe be due,
Truſts without fear, to merit, and to you.

DRAMATIS PERSONÆ.

MEN.

Mr. Honeywood,	Mr. Powell.
Croaker,	Mr. Shuter.
Lofty,	Mr. Woodward.
Sir William Honeywood,	Mr. Clarke.
Leontine,	Mr. Bensley.
Jarvis,	Mr. Dunstall.
Butler,	Mr. Cushing.
Bailiff,	Mr. R. Smith.
Dubardieu,	Mr. Holtom.
Poſtboy,	Mr. Quick.

WOMEN.

Miſs Richland,	Mrs. Bulkeley.
Olivia,	Mrs. Mattocks.
Mrs. Croaker,	Mrs. Pitt.
Garnet,	Mrs. Green.
Landlady,	Mrs. White.

SCENE, LONDON.

THE

GOOD-NATUR'D MAN.

ACT THE FIRST.

SCENE, an apartment in Young HONEYWOOD's house.

Enter Sir WILLIAM HONEYWOOD, JARVIS.

Sir WILLIAM.

GOOD Jarvis, make no apologies for this honeſt bluntneſs. Fidelity, like yours, is the beſt excuſe for every freedom.

JARVIS.

I can't help being blunt, and being very angry too, when I hear you talk of diſinheriting ſo good, ſo worthy a young gentleman as your nephew, my maſter. All the world loves him.

Sir WILLIAM.

Say rather, that he loves all the world; that is his fault.

JARVIS.

I'm ſure there is no part of it more dear to him than you are, though he has not ſeen you ſince he was a child,

Sir WILLIAM.

What ſignifies his affection to me; or how can I be proud of a place in a heart where every ſharper and coxcomb find an eaſy entrance?

JARVIS.

I grant you that he is rather too good-natur'd; that he's too much every man's man; that he laughs this minute with one, and cries the next with another: but whoſe inſtructions may he thank for all this?

Sir WILLIAM.

Not mine, ſure? My letters to him during my employment in Italy, taught him only that philoſophy which might prevent, not defend his errors.

JARVIS.

Faith, begging your honour's pardon, I'm ſorry they taught him any philoſophy at all; it has only ſerv'd to ſpoil him. This ſame philoſophy is a good horſe in the ſtable, but an arrant jade on a journey. For my own part, whenever I hear him mention the name on't, I'm always ſure he's going to play the fool.

Sir WILLIAM.

Don't let us aſcribe his faults to his philoſophy, I entreat you. No, Jarvis, his good nature ariſes rather from his fears of offending the importunate, than his deſire of making the deſerving happy.

JARVIS.

What it riſes from, I don't know. But, to be ſure, every body has it, that aſks it.

Sir

Sir WILLIAM.

Ay, or that does not aſk it. I have been now for ſome time a concealed ſpectator of his follies, and find them as boundleſs as his diſſipation.

JARVIS.

And yet, faith, he has ſome fine name or other for them all. He calls his extravagance, generoſity; and his truſting every body, univerſal benevolence. It was but laſt week he went ſecurity for a fellow whoſe face he ſcarce knew, and that he called an act of exalted mu—mu—munificence; ay, that was the name he gave it.

Sir WILLIAM.

And upon that I proceed, as my laſt effort, though with very little hopes to reclaim him. That very fellow has juſt abſconded, and I have taken up the ſecurity. Now, my intention is to involve him in fictitious diſtreſs, before he has plunged himſelf into real calamity. To arreſt him for that very debt, to clap an officer upon him, and then let him ſee which of his friends will come to his relief.

JARVIS.

Well, if I could but any way ſee him thoroughly vexed, every groan of his would be muſic to me; yet faith, I believe it impoſſible. I have tried to fret him myſelf every morning theſe three years; but, inſtead of being angry, he ſits as calmly to hear me ſcold, as he does to his hair-dreſſer.

Sir William.

We muſt try him once more, however, and I'll go this inſtant to put my ſcheme into execution; and I don't deſpair of ſucceeding, as, by your means, I can have frequent opportunities of being about him, without being known. What a pity it is, Jarvis, that any man's good-will to others ſhould produce ſo much neglect of himſelf, as to require correction? Yet, we muſt touch his weakneſſes with a delicate hand. There are ſome faults ſo nearly allied to excellence, that we can ſcarce weed out the vice without eradicating the virtue. [*Exit.*

Jarvis.

Well, go thy ways, Sir William Honeywood. It is not without reaſon that the world allows thee to be the beſt of men. But here comes his hopeful nephew; the ſtrange, good-natur'd, fooliſh, open-hearted—And yet, all his faults are ſuch that one loves him ſtill the better for them.

Enter Honeywood.

Honeywood.

Well, Jarvis, what meſſages from my friends this morning?

Jarvis.

You have no friends.

Honeywood.

Well; from my acquaintance then?

Jarvis.

JARVIS.

(Pulling out bills) A few of our uſual cards of compliment, that's all. This bill from your taylor; this from your mercer; and this from the little broker in Crooked-lane. He ſays he has been at a great deal of trouble to get back the money you borrowed.

HONEYWOOD.

That I don't know; but I'm ſure we were at a great deal of trouble in getting him to lend it.

JARVIS.

He has loſt all patience.

HONEYWOOD.

Then he has loſt a very good thing.

JARVIS.

There's that ten guineas you were ſending to the poor gentleman and his children in the Fleet. I believe that would ſtop his mouth, for a while at leaſt.

HONEYWOOD.

Ay, Jarvis, but what will fill their mouths in the mean time? Muſt I be cruel becauſe he happens to be importunate; and, to relieve his avarice, leave them to inſupportable diſtreſs?

JARVIS.

'Sdeath! Sir, the queſtion now is how to relieve yourſelf. Yourſelf—Hav'nt I reaſon to be out of my ſenſes, when I ſee things going at ſixes and ſevens?

HONEYWOOD.

Whatever reafon you may have for being out of your fenfes, I hope you'll allow that I'm not quite unreafonable for continuing in mine.

JARVIS.

You're the only man alive in your prefent fituation that could do fo—Every thing upon the wafte. There's Mifs Richland and her fine fortune gone already, and upon the point of being given to your rival.

HONEYWOOD.

I'm no man's rival.

JARVIS.

Your uncle in Italy preparing to difinherit you; your own fortune almoft fpent; and nothing but preffing creditors, falfe friends, and a pack of drunken fervants that your kindnefs has made unfit for any other family.

HONEYWOOD.

Then they have the more occafion for being in mine.

JARVIS.

Soh! What will you have done with him that I caught ftealing your plate in the pantry? In the fact; I caught him in the fact.

HONEYWOOD.

In the fact? If fo, I really think that we fhould pay him his wages, and turn him off.

JARVIS.

JARVIS.

He ſhall be turn'd off at Tyburn, the dog; we'll hang him, if it be only to frighten the reſt of the family.

HONEYWOOD.

No, Jarvis: it's enough that we have loſt what he has ſtolen, let us not add to it the loſs of a fellow creature!

JARVIS.

Very fine; well, here was the footman juſt now, to complain of the butler; he ſays he does moſt work, and ought to have moſt wages.

HONEYWOOD.

That's but juſt; though perhaps here comes the butler to complain of the footman.

JARVIS.

Ay, its the way with them all, from the ſcullion to the privy-counſellor. If they have a bad maſter, they keep quarrelling with him: if they have a good maſter, they keep quarrelling with one another.

Enter BUTLER, drunk.

BUTLER.

Sir, I'll not ſtay in the family with Jonathan you muſt part with him, or part with me, that's the ex-ex-expoſition of the matter, Sir.

HONEYWOOD.

Full and explicit enough. But what's his fault, good Philip?

BUTLER.

Sir, he's given to drinking, Sir, and I ſhall have my morals corrupted, by keeping ſuch company.

HONEYWOOD.

Ha! ha! He has ſuch a diverting way—

JARVIS.

O quite amuſing.

BUTLER.

I find my wines a-going, Sir; and liquors don't go without mouths, Sir; I hate a drunkard, Sir.

HONEYWOOD.

Well, well, Philip, I'll hear you upon that another time, ſo go to bed now.

JARVIS.

To bed! Let him go the devil.

BUTLER.

Begging your honour's pardon, and begging your pardon, maſter Jarvis, I'll not go to bed, nor to the devil neither. I have enough to do to mind my cellar. I forgot, your honour, Mr. Croaker is below. I came on purpoſe to tell you.

HONEYWOOD.

Why didn't you ſhew him up, blockhead?

BUTLER.

Shew him up, Sir! With all my heart, Sir. Up or down, all's one to me. *Exit.*

JARVIS.

Ay, we have one or other of that family in this houſe from morning till night. He comes on the

old

old affair, I ſuppoſe. The match between his ſon, that's juſt returned from Paris, and Miſs Richland, the young lady he's guardian to.

HONEYWOOD.

Perhaps ſo. Mr. Croaker, knowing my friendſhip for the young lady, has got it into his head that I can perſwade her to what I pleaſe.

JARVIS.

Ah! if you loved yourſelf but half as well as ſhe loves you, we ſhould ſoon ſee a marriage that would ſet all things to rights again.

HONEYWOOD.

Love me! Sure, Jarvis, you dream. No, no; her intimacy with me never amounted to more than friendſhip—mere friendſhip. That ſhe is the moſt lovely woman that ever warm'd the human heart with deſire, I own. But never let me harbour a thought of making her unhappy, by a connection with one ſo unworthy her merits as I am. No, Jarvis, it ſhall be my ſtudy to ſerve her, even in ſpite of my wiſhes; and to ſecure her happineſs, though it deſtroys my own.

JARVIS.

Was ever the like! I want patience.

HONEYWOOD.

Beſides, Jarvis, though I could obtain Miſs Richland's conſent, do you think I could ſucceed with her guardian, or Mrs. Croaker his wife; who, tho' both very fine in their way, are yet a little oppoſite in their diſpoſitions you know.

JARVIS.

JARVIS.

Oppoſite enough, heaven knows; the very reverſe of each other; ſhe all laugh and no joke; he always complaining and never ſorrowful; a fretful poor ſoul that has a new diſtreſs for every hour in the four and twenty—

HONEYWOOD.

Huſh, huſh, he's coming up, he'll hear you.

JARVIS.

One who's voice is a paſſing bell—

HONEYWOOD.

Well, well, go, do.

JARVIS.

A raven that bodes nothing but miſchief; a coffin and croſs bones; a bundle of rue; a ſprig of deadly night ſhade; a—*(Honeywood ſtopping his mouth, at laſt puſhes him off.)* [*Exit* Jarvis.

HONEYWOOD.

I muſt own my old monitor is not entirely wrong. There is ſomething in my friend Croaker's converſation that quite depreſſes me. His very mirth is an antidote to all gaiety, and his appearance has a ſtronger effect on my ſpirits than an undertaker's ſhop.—Mr. Croaker, this is ſuch a ſatisfaction—

Enter CROAKER.

CROAKER.

A pleaſant morning to Mr. Honeywood, and many of them. How is this! you look moſt ſhockingly

ingly to day, my dear friend. I hope this weather does not affect your ſpirits. To be ſure, if this weather continues—I ſay nothing—But God ſend we be all better this day three months.

HONEYWOOD.

I heartily concur in the wiſh, though I own not in your apprehenſions.

CROAKER.

May be not! indeed what ſignifies what weather we have in a country going to ruin like ours? taxes riſing and trade falling. Money flying out of the kingdom, and Jeſuits ſwarming into it. I know at this time no leſs than an hundred and twenty-ſeven Jeſuits between Charing-croſs and Temple-bar.

HONEYWOOD.

The Jeſuits will ſcarce pervert you or me, I ſhould hope.

CROAKER.

May be not. Indeed what ſignifies whom they pervert in a country that has ſcarce any religion to loſe? I'm only afraid for our wives and daughters.

HONEYWOOD.

I have no apprehenſions for the ladies, I aſſure you.

CROAKER.

May be not. Indeed what ſignifies whether they be perverted or no? the women in my time were good for ſomething. I have ſeen a lady dreſt from top to toe in her own manufactures formerly. But now

now a-days the devil a thing of their own manufactures about them, except their faces.

HONEYWOOD.

But, however thefe faults may be practifed abroad, you don't find them at home, either with Mrs. Croaker, Olivia, or Mifs Richland.

CROAKER.

The beft of them will never be canoniz'd for a faint when fhe's dead. By the bye, my dear friend, I don't find this match between Mifs Richland and my fon much relifhed, either by one fide or t'other.

HONEYWOOD.

I thought otherwife.

CROAKER.

Ah, Mr. Honeywood, a little of your fine ferious advice to the young lady might go far: I know fhe has a very exalted opinion of your underftanding.

HONEYWOOD.

But would not that be ufurping an authority that more properly belongs to yourfelf?

CROAKER.

My dear friend, you know but little of my authority at home. People think, indeed, becaufe they fee me come out in a morning thus, with a pleafant face, and to make my friends merry, that all's well within. But I have cares that would break an heart of ftone. My wife has fo encroached upon every one of my privileges, that I'm now no more than a mere lodger in my own houfe.

Ho-

HONEYWOOD.

But a little ſpirit exerted on your ſide might perhaps reſtore your authority.

CROAKER.

No, though I had the ſpirit of a lion! I do rouze ſometimes. But what then! always haggling and haggling. A man is tired of getting the better before his wiſe is tired of loſing the victory.

HONEYWOOD.

It's a melancholy conſideration indeed, that our chief comforts often produce our greateſt anxieties, and that an encreaſe of our poſſeſſions is but an inlet to new diſquietudes.

CROAKER.

Ah, my dear friend, theſe were the very words of poor Dick Doleful to me not a week before he made away with himſelf. Indeed, Mr. Honeywood, I never ſee you but you put me in mind of poor— Dick. Ah there was merit neglected for you! and ſo true a friend; we lov'd each other for thirty years, and yet he never aſked me to lend him a ſingle farthing.

HONEYWOOD.

Pray what could induce him to commit ſo raſh an action at laſt?

CROAKER.

I don't know, ſome people were malicious enough to ſay it was keeping company with me; becauſe we uſed to meet now and then and open our hearts to each other. To be ſure I loved to hear him talk, and he loved to hear me talk; poor dear Dick. He us'd to ſay that Croaker rhim'd to joker; and ſo we us'd to laugh—Poor Dick. *(Going to cry.)*

HONEYWOOD.

His fate affects me.

CROAKER.

Ay, he grew ſick of this miſerable life, where we do nothing but eat and grow hungry, dreſs and undreſs, get up and lie down; while reaſon, that ſhould watch like a nurſe by our ſide, falls as faſt aſleep as we do.

HONEYWOOD.

To ſay truth, if we compare that part of life which is to come, by that which we have paſt, the proſpect is hideous.

CROAKER.

Life at the greateſt and beſt is but a froward child, that muſt be humour'd and coax'd a little till it falls aſleep, and then all the care is over.

HONEYWOOD.

Very true, Sir, nothing can exceed the vanity of our exiſtence, but the folly of our purſuits. We wept when we came into the world, and every day tells us why.

CROAKER.

Ah, my dear friend, it is a perfect ſatisfaction to be miſerable with you. My ſon Leontine ſhan't loſe the benefit of ſuch fine converſation. I'll juſt ſtep

home

home for him. I am willing to ſhew him ſo much ſerioufneſs in one ſcarce older than himſelf—And what if I bring my laſt letter to the Gazetteer on the encreaſe and progreſs of earthquakes? It will amuſe us, I promiſe you. I there prove how the late earthquake is coming round to pay us another viſit from London to Liſbon, from Liſbon to the Canary Iſlands, from the Canary Iſlands to Palmyra, from Palmyra to Conſtantinople, and ſo from Conſtantinople back to London again. [*Exit.*

HONEYWOOD.

Poor Croaker! his ſituation deſerves the utmoſt pity.. I ſhall ſcarce recover my ſpirits theſe three days. Sure to live upon ſuch terms is worſe than death itſelf. And yet, when I conſider my own ſituation, a broken fortune, an hopeleſs paſſion, friends in diſtreſs; the wiſh but not the power to ſerve them——*(pauſing and ſighing.)*

Enter BUTLER.

BUTLER.

More company below, Sir: Mrs. Croaker and Miſs Richland; ſhall I ſhew them up? but they're ſhewing up themſelves. [*Exit.*

Enter Mrs. CROAKER and Miſs RICHLAND.

Miſs RICHLAND.

You're always in ſuch ſpirits.

Mrs. CROAKER.

We have juſt come, my dear Honeywood, from the auction. There was the old deaf dowager, as

 uſual,

uſual, bidding like a fury againſt herſelf. And then ſo curious in antiques! herſelf the moſt genuine piece of antiquity in the whole collection.

HONEYWOOD.

Excuſe me, ladies, if ſome uneaſineſs from friendſhip makes me unfit to ſhare in this good humour: I know you'll pardon me.

Mrs. CROAKER.

I vow he ſeems as melancholy as if he had taken a doſe of my huſband this morning. Well, if Richland here can pardon you, I muſt.

Miſs RICHLAND.

You would ſeem to inſinuate, madam, that I have particular reaſons for being diſpoſed to refuſe it.

Mrs. CROAKER.

Whatever I inſinuate, my dear, don't be ſo ready to wiſh an explanation.

Miſs RICHLAND.

I own I ſhould be ſorry, Mr. Honeywood's long friendſhip and mine ſhould be miſunderſtood.

HONEYWOOD.

There's no anſwering for others, madam. But I hope you'll never find me preſuming to offer more than the moſt delicate friendſhip may readily allow.

Miſs RICHLAND.

And I ſhall be prouder of ſuch a tribute from you than the moſt paſſionate profeſſions from others.

Ho-

HONEYWOOD.

My own ſentiments, madam: friendſhip is a diſ-intereſted commerce between equals; love, an ab-ject intercourſe between tyrants and ſlaves.

Miſs RICHLAND.

And, without a compliment, I know none more diſintereſted, or more capable of friendſhip than Mr. Honeywood.

Mrs. CROAKER.

And, indeed, I know nobody that has more friends, at leaſt among the ladies. Miſs Fruzz, Miſs Odbody, and Miſs Winterbottom praiſe him in all companies. As for Miſs Biddy Bundle, ſhe's his profeſſed admirer.

Miſs RICHLAND.

Indeed! an admirer! I did not know, Sir, you were ſuch a favourite there. But is ſhe ſeriouſly ſo handſome? Is ſhe the mighty thing talked of?

HONEYWOOD.

The town, madam, ſeldom begins to praiſe a lady's beauty, till ſhe's beginning to loſe it. (*Smiling.*)

Mrs. CROAKER.

But ſhe's reſolv'd never to loſe it, it ſeems. For, as her natural face decays, her ſkill improves in making the artificial one. Well, nothing diverts me more than one of thoſe fine, old, dreſſy things, who thinks to conceal her age, by every where expoſing her perſon; ſticking herſelf up in the front of a ſide-box; trailing through a minuet at Almack's; and then, in the public gardens, looking for all the world like one of the painted ruins of the place.

HONEYWOOD.

Every age has its admirers, ladies. While you, perhaps, are trading among the warmer climates of youth; there ought to be ſome to carry on an uſeful commerce in the frozen latitudes beyond fifty.

Miſs RICHLAND.

But, then, the mortifications they muſt ſuffer, before they can be fitted out for traffic. I have ſeen one of them fret an whole morning at her hair-dreſſer, when all the fault was her face.

HONEYWOOD.

And yet, I'll engage, has carried that face at laſt to a very good market. This good-natur'd town, madam, has huſbands, like ſpectacles, to fit every age, from fifteen to fourſcore.

Mrs. CROAKER.

Well, you're a dear good-natur'd creature. But you know you're engaged with us this morning upon a ſtrolling party. I want to ſhew Olivia the town, and the things; I believe I ſhall have buſineſs for you for the whole day.

HONEYWOOD.

I am ſorry, madam, I have an appointment with Mr. Croaker, which it is impoſſible to put off.

Mrs.

Mrs. Croaker.

What! with my huſband! then I'm reſolved to take no refuſal. Nay, I proteſt you muſt. You know I never laugh ſo much as with you.

Honeywood.

Why, if I muſt, I muſt. I'll ſwear you have put me into ſuch ſpirits. Well, do you find jeſt, and I'll find laugh, I promiſe you. We'll wait for the chariot in the next room. [*Exeunt.*

Enter Leontine and Olivia.

Leontine.

There they go, thoughtleſs and happy. My deareſt Olivia, what would I give to ſee you capable of ſharing in their amuſements, and as cheerful as they are?

Olivia.

How, my Leontine, how can I be cheerful, when I have ſo many terrors to oppreſs me? the fear of being detected by this family, and the apprehenſions of a cenſuring world, when I muſt be detected—

Leontine.

The world! my love, what can it ſay? At worſt it can only ſay that, being compelled by a mercenary guardian to embrace a life you diſliked, you formed a reſolution of flying with the man of your choice; that you confided in his honour, and took refuge in my father's houſe; the only one where your's could remain without cenſure.

OLIVIA.

But consider, Leontine, your disobedience and my indiscretion: your being sent to France to bring home a sister; and, instead of a sister, bringing home——

LEONTINE.

One dearer than a thousand sisters. One that I am convinc'd will be equally dear, to the rest of the family, when she comes to be known.

OLIVIA.

And that, I fear, will shortly be.

LEONTINE.

Impossible, 'till we ourselves think proper to make the discovery. My sister, you know, has been with her aunt, at Lyons, since she was a child, and you find every creature in the family takes you for her.

OLIVIA.

But mayn't she write, mayn't her aunt write?

LEONTINE.

Her aunt scarce ever writes, and all my sister's letters are directed to me.

OLIVIA.

But won't your refusing Miss Richland, for whom you know the old gentleman intends you, create a suspicion?

LEONTINE.

There, there's my master-stroke. I have resolved not to refuse her; nay, an hour hence I have consented to go with my father, to make her an offer of my heart and fortune.

OLI-

OLIVIA.

Your heart and fortune!

LEONTINE.

Don't be alarm'd, my dearest. Can Olivia think so meanly of my honour, or my love, as to suppose I could ever hope for happiness from any but her? No, my Olivia, neither the force, nor, permit me to add, the delicacy of my passion, leave any room to suspect me. I only offer Miss Richland an heart, I am convinc'd she will refuse; as I am confident, that, without knowing it, her affections are fixed upon Mr. Honeywood

OLIVIA.

Mr. Honeywood! You'll excuse my apprehensions; but when your merits come to be put in the balance—

LEONTINE.

You view them with too much partiality. However, by making this offer, I shew a seeming compliance with my father's command; and perhaps, upon her refusal, I may have his consent to chuse for myself.

OLIVIA.

Well, I submit. And yet, my Leontine, I own, I shall envy her, even your pretended addresses. I consider every look, every expression of your esteem, as due only to me. This is folly perhaps: I allow it: but it is natural to suppose, that merit which has made an impreſſion on one's own heart, may be powerful over that of another.

LEONTINE.

Don't, my life's treaſure, don't let us make imaginary evils, when you know we have ſo many real ones to encounter. At worſt, you know, if Miſs Richland ſhould conſent, or my father refuſe his pardon, it can but end in a trip to Scotland; and—

Enter CROAKER.

CROAKER.

Where have you been, boy? I have been ſeeking you. My friend Honeywood here, has been ſaying ſuch comfortable things. Ah! he's an example indeed. Where is he? I left him here.

LEONTINE.

Sir, I believe you may ſee him, and hear him too in the next room: he's preparing to go out with the ladies.

CROAKER.

Good gracious, can I believe my eyes or my ears! I'm ſtruck dumb with his vivacity, and ſtunn'd with the loudneſs of his laugh. Was there ever ſuch a transformation! *(A laugh behind the ſcenes, Croaker mimics it.)* Ha! ha! ha! there it goes: a plague take their balderdaſh; yet I could expect nothing leſs, when my precious wife was of the party. On my conſcience, I believe, ſhe could ſpread an horſe-laugh through the pews of a tabernacle.

LEON-

LEONTINE.

Since you find ſo many objections to a wife, ſir, how can you be ſo earneſt in recommending one to me?

CROAKER.

I have told you, and tell you again, boy, that Miſs Richland's fortune muſt not go out of the family; one may find comfort in the money, whatever one does in the wife.

LEONTINE.

But, Sir, though, in obedience to your deſire, I am ready to marry her; it may be poſſible, ſhe has no inclination to me.

CROAKER.

I'll tell you once for all how it ſtands. A good part of Miſs Richland's large fortune conſiſts in a claim upon government, which my good friend, Mr. Lofty, aſſures me the treaſury will allow. One half of this ſhe is to forfeit, by her father's will, in caſe ſhe refuſes to marry you. So, if ſhe rejects you, we ſeize half her fortune; if ſhe accepts you, we ſeize the whole, and a fine girl into the bargain.

LEONTINE.

But, Sir, if you will but liſten to reaſon——

CROAKER.

Come, then, produce your reaſons. I tell you I'm fix'd, determined, ſo now produce your reaſons. When I'm determined, I always liſten to reaſon, becauſe it can then do no harm.

LEON-

LEONTINE.

You have alledged that a mutual choice was the firſt requiſite in matrimonial happineſs.

CROAKER.

Well, and you have both of you a mutual choice. She has her choice—to marry you, or loſe half her fortune; and you have your choice—to marry her, or pack out of doors without any fortune at all.

LEONTINE.

An only ſon, Sir, might expect more indulgence.

CROAKER.

An only father, Sir, might expect more obedience; beſides, has not your ſiſter here, that never diſobliged me in her life, as good a right as you? He's a ſad dog, Livy, my dear, and would take all from you. But he ſhan't, I tell you he ſhan't, for you ſhall have your ſhare.

OLIVIA.

Dear Sir, I wiſh you'd be convinced that I can never be happy in any addition to my fortune, which is taken from his.

CROAKER.

Well, well, it's a good child, ſo ſay no more; but come with me, and we ſhall ſee ſomething that will give us a great deal of pleaſure, I promiſe you; old Ruggins, the curry-comb-maker, lying in ſtate; I'm told he makes a very handſome corpſe, and becomes his coffin prodigiouſly. He was an intimate friend of mine, and theſe are friendly things we ought to do for each other. [*Exeunt.*

ACT

ACT THE SECOND.

SCENE, CROAKER's Houſe.

Miſs RICHLAND, GARNET.

Miſs RICHLAND.

OLIVIA not his ſiſter? Olivia not Leontine's ſiſter? You amaze me!

GARNET.

No more his ſiſter than I am; I had it all from his own ſervant; I can get any thing from that quarter.

Miſs RICHLAND.

But how? Tell me again, Garnet.

GARNET.

Why, madam, as I told you before, inſtead of going to Lyons, to bring home his ſiſter, who has been there with her aunt theſe ten years; he never went further than Paris; there he ſaw and fell in love with this young lady, by the bye, of a prodigious family.

Miſs RICHLAND.

And brought her home to my guardian, as his daughter?

GAR-

GARNET.

Yes, and his daughter ſhe will be. If he don't conſent to their marriage, they talk of trying what a Scotch parſon can do.

Miſs RICHLAND.

Well, I own they have deceived me—And ſo demurely as Olivia carried it to!—Would you believe it, Garnet, I told her all my ſecrets; and yet the ſly cheat concealed all this from me?

GARNET.

And, upon my word, madam, I don't much blame her; ſhe was loth to truſt one with her ſecrets, that was ſo very bad at keeping her own.

Miſs RICHLAND.

But, to add to their deceit, the young gentleman, it ſeems, pretends to make me ſerious propoſals. My guardian and he are to be here preſently, to open the affair in form. You know I am to loſe half my fortune if I refuſe him.

GARNET.

Yet, what can you do? For being, as you are, in love with Mr. Honeywood, madam—

Miſs RICHLAND.

How! idiot; what do you mean? In love with Mr. Honeywood! Is this to provoke me?

GARNET.

That is, madam, in friendſhip with him; I meant nothing more than friendſhip, as I hope to be married; nothing more.

Miſs Richland.

Well, no more of this! As to my guardian, and his ſon, they ſhall find me prepared to receive them; I'm reſolved to accept their propoſal with ſeeming pleaſure, to mortify them by compliance, and ſo throw the refuſal at laſt upon them.

Garnet.

Delicious! and that will ſecure your whole fortune to yourſelf. Well, who could have thought ſo innocent a face could cover ſo much cuteneſs!

Miſs Richland.

Why, girl, I only oppoſe my prudence to their cunning, and practiſe a leſſon they have taught me againſt themſelves.

Garnet.

Then you're likely not long to want employment, for here they come, and in cloſe conference.

Enter Croaker, Leontine.

Leontine.

Excuſe me, Sir, if I ſeem to heſitate upon the point of putting to the lady ſo important a queſtion.

Croaker.

Lord! good Sir, moderate your fears; you're ſo plaguy ſhy, that one would think you had changed ſexes. I tell you we muſt have the half or the whole. Come, let me ſee with what ſpirit you begin? Well, why don't you? Eh! What? Well then

then—I muſt, it ſeems—Miſs Richland, my dear, I believe you gueſs at our buſineſs; an affair which my ſon here comes to open, that nearly concerns your happineſs.

Miſs RICHLAND.

Sir, I ſhould be ungrateful not to be pleaſed with any thing that comes recommended by you.

CROAKER.

How, boy, could you deſire a finer opening? Why don't you begin, I ſay? (*To Leont.*)

LEONTINE.

'Tis true, madam, my father, madam, has ſome intentions—hem—of explaining an affair—which—himſelf—can beſt explain, madam.

CROAKER.

Yes, my dear; it comes intirely from my ſon; it's all a requeſt of his own, madam. And I will permit him to make the beſt of it.

LEONTINE.

The whole affair is only this, madam; my father has a propoſal to make, which he inſiſts none but himſelf ſhall deliver.

CROAKER.

My mind miſgives me, the fellow will never be brought on. (*Aſide.*) In ſhort, madam, you ſee before you one that loves you; one whoſe whole happineſs is all in you.

Miſs

Miſs RICHLAND.

I never had any doubts of your regard, Sir; and I hope you can have none of my duty.

CROAKER.

That's not the thing, my little ſweeting; my love! No, no, another gueſs lover than I; there he ſtands, madam, his very looks declare the force of his paſſion—Call up a look you dog (*Aſide*)—But then, had you ſeen him, as I have, weeping, ſpeaking ſoliloquies and blank verſe, ſometimes melancholy, and ſometimes abſent—

Miſs RICHLAND.

I fear, Sir, he's abſent now; or ſuch a declaration would have come moſt properly from himſelf.

CROAKER.

Himſelf! madam, he would die before he could make ſuch a confeſſion; and if he had not a channel for his paſſion through me, it would ere now have drowned his underſtanding.

Miſs RICHLAND.

I muſt grant, Sir, there are attractions in modeſt diffidence above the force of words. A ſilent addreſs is the genuine eloquence of ſincerity.

CROAKER.

Madam, he has forgot to ſpeak any other language; ſilence is become his mother tongue.

Miſs RICHLAND.

And it muſt be confeſſed, Sir, it ſpeaks very powerfully in his favour. And yet I ſhall be

thought

thought too forward in making ſuch a confeſſion; ſhan't I, Mr. Leontine?

LEONTINE.

Confuſion! my reſerve will undo me. But, if modeſty attracts her, impudence may diſguſt her. I'll try. (*Aſide.*) Don't imagine from my ſilence, madam, that I want a due ſenſe of the honour and happineſs intended me. My father, madam, tells me, your humble ſervant is not totally indifferent to you. He admires you; I adore you; and when we come together, upon my ſoul I believe we ſhall be the happieſt couple in all St. James's.

Miſs RICHLAND.

If I could flatter myſelf, you thought as you ſpeak, Sir—

LEONTINE.

Doubt my ſincerity, madam? By your dear ſelf I ſwear. Aſk the brave, if they deſire glory? aſk cowards, if they covet ſafety——

CROAKER.

Well, well, no more queſtions about it.

LEONTINE.

Aſk the ſick, if they long for health? aſk miſers, if they love money? aſk——

CROAKER.

Aſk a fool, if he can talk nonſenſe! What's come over the boy? What ſignifies aſking, when there's not a ſoul to give you an anſwer? If you would

would aſk to the purpoſe, aſk this lady's conſent to make you happy.

Miſs RICHLAND.

Why indeed, Sir, his uncommon ardour almoſt compels me—forces me to comply. And yet I'm afraid he'll deſpiſe a conqueſt gained with too much eaſe: won't you, Mr. Leontine?

LEONTINE.

Confuſion! *(Aſide.)* Oh, by no means, madam, by no means. And yet, madam, you talked of force. There is nothing I would avoid ſo much as compulſion in a thing of this kind. No, madam, I will ſtill be generous, and leave you at liberty to refuſe.

CROAKER.

But I tell you, Sir, the lady is not at liberty. It's a match. You ſee ſhe ſays nothing. Silence gives conſent.

LEONTINE.

But, Sir, ſhe talked of force. Conſider, Sir, the cruelty of conſtraining her inclinations.

CROAKER.

But I ſay there's no cruelty. Don't you know, blockhead, that girls have always a roundabout way of ſaying yes before company? So get you both gone together into the next room, and hang him that interrupts the tender explanation. Get you gone, I ſay; I'll not hear a word.

LEONTINE.

But, Sir, I muſt beg leave to inſiſt—

CROAKER.

Get off, you puppy, or I'll beg leave to inſiſt upon knocking you down. Stupid whelp! But I don't wonder, the boy takes entirely after his mother [*Exeunt Miſs* Rich. *and* Leont.

Enter Mrs. CROAKER.

Mrs. CROAKER.

Mr. Croaker, I bring you ſomething, my dear, that I believe will make you ſmile.

CROAKER.

I'll hold you a guinea of that, my dear.

Mrs. CROAKER.

A letter; and, as I knew the hand, I ventur'd to open it.

CROAKER.

And how can you expect your breaking open my letters ſhould give me pleaſure?

Mrs. CROAKER.

Poo, it's from your ſiſter at Lyons, and contains good news: read it.

CROAKER.

What a Frenchified cover is here! That ſiſter of mine has ſome good qualities, but I could never teach her to fold a letter.

Mrs. CROAKER.

Fold a fiddleſtick. Read what it contains.

CROAKER.

CROAKER, reading.

"DEAR NICK,

"AN Engliſh gentleman, of large fortune, has "for ſome time made private, though honourable "propoſals to your daughter Olivia. They love "each other tenderly, and I find ſhe has conſented, "without letting any of the family know, to crown "his addreſſes. As ſuch good offers don't come "every day, your own good ſenſe, his large fortune, "and family conſiderations, will induce you to for-"give her.

"Yours ever,

"RACHAEL CROAKER."

My daughter, Olivia, privately contracted to a man of large fortune! This is good news, indeed. My heart never foretold me of this. And yet, how ſlily the little baggage has carried it ſince ſhe came home. Not a word on't to the old ones for the world. Yet, I thought, I ſaw ſomething ſhe wanted to conceal.

Mrs. CROAKER.

Well, if they have concealed their amour, they ſhan't conceal their wedding; that ſhall be public, I'm reſolved.

CROAKER.

I tell thee, woman, the wedding is the moſt fooliſh part of the ceremony. I can never get this woman to think of the more ſerious part of the nuptial engagement.

Mrs. CROAKER.

What, would you have me think of their funeral? But come, tell me, my dear, don't you owe more to me than you care to confefs? Would you have ever been known to Mr. Lofty, who has undertaken Mifs Richland's claim at the treafury, but for me? Who was it firft made him an acquaintance at lady Shabbaroon's rout? Who got him to promife us his intereft? Is not he a back-ftairs favourite, one that can do what he pleafes with thofe that do what they pleafe? Is not he an acquaintance that all your groaning and lamentations could never have got us?

CROAKER.

He is a man of importance, I grant you. And yet, what amazes me is, that while he is giving away places to all the world, he can't get one for himfelf.

Mrs. CROAKER.

That perhaps may be owing to his nicety. Great men are not eafily fatisfied.

Enter FRENCH SERVANT.

SERVANT.

An expreffe from Monfieur Lofty. He vil be vait upon your honour's inftrammant. He be only giving four five inftruction, read two three memorial, call upon von ambaffadeur. He vil be vid you in one tree minutes.

Mrs.

Mrs. CROAKER.

You ſee now, my dear. What an extenſive department! Well, friend, let your maſter know, that we are extremely honoured by this honour. Was there any thing ever in a higher ſtyle of breeding! All meſſages among the great are now done by expreſs.

CROAKER.

To be ſure, no man does little things with more ſolemnity, or claims more reſpect than he. But he's in the right on't. In our bad world, reſpect is given, where reſpect is claim'd.

Mrs. CROAKER.

Never mind the world, my dear; you were never in a pleaſanter place in your life. Let us now think of receiving him with proper reſpect (*a loud rapping at the door*) and there he is by the thundering rap.

CROAKER.

Ay, verily, there he is; as cloſe upon the heels of his own expreſs, as an indorſement upon the back of a bill. Well, I'll leave you to receive him, whilſt I go to chide my little Olivia for intending to ſteal a marriage without mine, or her aunt's conſent. I muſt ſeem to be angry, or ſhe too may begin to deſpiſe my authority. [*Exit.*

Enter LOFTY, ſpeaking to his Servant.

LOFTY.

" And if the Venetian ambaſſador, or that teazing creature the marquis, ſhould call, I'm not at home. Dam'me, I'll be pack-horſe to none of them." My dear madam, I have juſt ſnatched a moment—" And if the expreſſes to his grace be ready, let them be ſent off; they're of importance." Madam, I aſk a thouſand pardons.

Mrs. CROAKER.

Sir, this honour——

LOFTY.

" And Dubardieu! if the perſon calls about the commiſſion, let him know that it is made out. As for lord Cumbercourt's ſtale requeſt, it can keep cold: you underſtand me." Madam, I aſk ten thouſand pardons.

Mrs. CROAKER.

Sir, this honour——

LOFTY.

" And, Dubardieu! if the man comes from the Corniſh borough, you muſt do him; you muſt do him, I ſay." Madam, I aſk ten thouſand pardons. " And if the Ruſſian—ambaſſador calls: but he will ſcarce call to-day, I believe." And now, madam, I have juſt got time to expreſs my happineſs in having the honour of being permitted to profeſs myſelf your moſt obedient humble ſervant.

Mrs.

Mrs. Croaker.

Sir, the happineſs and honour are all mine; and yet, I'm only robbing the public while I detain you.

Lofty.

Sink the public, madam, when the fair are to be attended. Ah, could all my hours be ſo charmingly devoted! Sincerely, don't you pity us poor creatures in affairs? Thus it is eternally; ſolicited for places here, teized for penſions there, and courted every where. I know you pity me. Yes, I ſee you do.

Mrs. Croaker.

Excuſe me, Sir. "Toils of empires pleaſures are," as Waller ſays.

Lofty.

Waller, Waller; is he of the houſe?

Mrs. Croaker.

The modern poet of that name, Sir.

Lofty.

Oh, a modern! We men of buſineſs deſpiſe the moderns; and as for the ancients, we have no time to read them. Poetry is a pretty thing enough for our wives and daughters; but not for us. Why now, here I ſtand that know nothing of books. I ſay, madam, I know nothing of books; and yet, I believe, upon a land carriage fiſhery, a ſtamp act, or a jag-hire, I can talk my two hours without feeling the want of them.

Mrs. Croaker.

The world is no ſtranger to Mr. Lofty's eminence in every capacity.

Lofty.

I vow to gad, madam, you make me bluſh. I'm nothing, nothing, nothing in the world; a mere obſcure gentleman. To be ſure, indeed, one or two of the preſent miniſters are pleaſed to repreſent me as a formidable man. I know they are pleaſed to be-ſpatter me at all their little dirty levees. Yet, upon my ſoul, I wonder what they ſee in me to treat me ſo! Meaſures, not men, have always been my mark; and I vow, by all that's honourable, my reſentment has never done the men, as mere men, any manner of harm—that is as mere men.

Mrs. Croaker.

What importance, and yet what modeſty!

Lofty.

Oh, if you talk of modeſty, madam! there I own, I'm acceſſible to praiſe: modeſty is my foible: it was ſo, the duke of Brentford uſed to ſay of me. "I love Jack Lofty, he uſed to ſay:" no man has a finer knowledge of things; quite a man of information; and when he ſpeaks upon his legs, by the Lord he's prodigious, he ſcouts them; and yet all men have their faults; too much modeſty is his, ſays his grace.

Mrs. CROAKER.

And yet, I dare ſay, you don't want aſſurance when you come to ſolicit for your friends.

LOFTY.

O, there indeed I'm in bronze. Apropos! I have juſt been mentioning Miſs Richland's caſe to a certain perſonage; we muſt name no names. When I aſk, I'm not to be put off, madam. No, no, I take my friend by the button. A fine girl, Sir; great juſtice in her caſe. A friend of mine. Borough intereſt. Buſineſs muſt be done, Mr. Secretary. I ſay, Mr. Secretary, her buſineſs muſt be done, Sir. That's my way, madam.

Mrs. CROAKER.

Bleſs me! you ſaid all this to the ſecretary of ſtate, did you?

LOFTY.

I did not ſay the ſecretary, did I? Well, curſe it, ſince you have found me out I will not deny it. It was to the ſecretary.

Mrs. CROAKER.

This was going to the fountain head at once, not applying to the underſtrappers, as Mr. Honeywood would have had us.

LOFTY.

Honeywood! he! he! He was, indeed, a fine ſolicitor. I ſuppoſe you have heard what has juſt happened to him?

Mrs.

Mrs. CROAKER.

Poor dear man ; no accident, I hope.

LOFTY.

Undone, madam, that's all. His creditors have taken him into cuſtody. A priſoner in his own houſe.

Mrs. CROAKER.

A priſoner in his own houſe! How! At this very time! I'm quite unhappy for him.

LOFTY.

Why ſo am I. The man, to be ſure, was immenſely good-natur'd. But then I could never find that he had any thing in him.

Mrs. CROAKER.

His manner, to be ſure, was exceſſive harmleſs; ſome, indeed, thought it a little dull. For my part, I always concealed my opinion.

LOFTY.

It can't be concealed, madam; the man was dull, dull as the laſt new comedy! A poor impracticable creature? I tried once or twice to know if he was fit for buſineſs; but he had ſcarce talents to be groom-porter to an orange barrow.

Mrs. CROAKER.

How differently does Miſs Richland think of him! For, I believe, with all his faults, ſhe loves him.

LOFTY.

Loves him! Does ſhe? You ſhould cure her of that by all means. Let me ſee; what if ſhe were

ſent

ſent to him this inſtant, in his preſent doleful ſituation? My life for it, that works her cure. Diſtreſs is a perfect antidote to love. Suppoſe we join her in the next room? Miſs Richland is a fine girl, has a fine fortune, and muſt not be thrown away. Upon my honour, madam, I have a regard for Miſs Richland; and rather than ſhe ſhould be thrown away, I ſhould think it no indignity to marry her myſelf. [*Exeunt.*

Enter OLIVIA and LEONTINE.

LEONTINE.

And yet, truſt me, Olivia, I had every reaſon to expect Miſs Richland's refuſal, as I did every thing in my power to deſerve it. Her indelicacy ſurpriſes me!

OLIVIA.

Sure, Leontine, there's nothing ſo indelicate in being ſenſible of your merit. If ſo, I fear, I ſhall be the moſt guilty thing alive.

LEONTINE.

But you miſtake, my dear. The ſame attention I uſed to advance my merit with you, I practiſed to leſſen it with her. What more could I do?

OLIVIA.

Let us now rather conſider what's to be done. We have both diſſembled too long—I have always been aſhamed—I am now quite weary of it. Sure

I could

I could never have undergone ſo much for any other but you.

LEONTINE.

And you ſhall find my gratitude equal to your kindeſt compliance. Though our friends ſhould totally forſake us, Olivia, we can draw upon content for the deficiencies of fortune.

OLIVIA.

Then why ſhould we defer our ſcheme of humble happineſs, when it is now in our power? I may be the favourite of your father, it is true; but can it ever be thought, that his preſent kindneſs to a ſuppoſed child, will continue to a known deceiver?

LEONTINE.

I have many reaſons to believe it will. As his attachments are but few, they are laſting. His own marriage was a private one, as ours may be. Beſides, I have ſounded him already at a diſtance, and find all his anſwers exactly to our wiſh. Nay, by an expreſſion or two that dropped from him, I am induced to think he knows of this affair.

OLIVIA.

Indeed! But that would be an happineſs too great to be expected.

LEONTINE.

However it be, I'm certain you have power over him; and am perſuaded, if you informed him of our ſituation, that he would be diſpoſed to pardon it.

OLIVIA.

OLIVIA.

You had equal expectations, Leontine, from your last scheme with Miss Richland, which you find has succeeded most wretchedly.

LEONTINE.

And that's the best reason for trying another.

OLIVIA.

If it must be so, I submit.

LEONTINE.

As we could wish, he comes this way. Now, my dearest Olivia, be resolute. I'll just retire within hearing, to come in at a proper time, either to share your danger, or confirm your victory. [*Exit.*

Enter CROAKER.

CROAKER.

Yes, I must forgive her; and yet not too easily, neither. It will be proper to keep up the decorums of resentment a little, if it be only to impress her with an idea of my authority.

OLIVIA.

How I tremble to approach him!—Might I presume, Sir—If I interrupt you—

CROAKER.

No, child, where I have an affection, it is not a little thing that can interrupt me. Affection gets over little things.

OLIVIA.

OLIVIA.

Sir, you're too kind. I'm ſenſible how ill I deſerve this partiality. Yet, heaven knows, there is nothing I would not do to gain it.

CROAKER.

And you have but too well ſucceeded, you little huſſey, you. With thoſe endearing ways of yours, on my conſcience, I could be brought to forgive any thing, unleſs it were a very great offence indeed.

OLIVIA.

But mine is ſuch an offence—When you know my guilt—Yes, you ſhall know it, though I feel the greateſt pain in the confeſſion.

CROAKER.

Why then, if it be ſo very great a pain, you may ſpare yourſelf the trouble; for I know every ſyllable of the matter before you begin.

OLIVIA.

Indeed! Then I'm undone.

CROAKER.

Ay, miſs, you wanted to ſteal a match, without letting me know it, did you? But, I'm not worth being conſulted, I ſuppoſe, when there's to be a marriage in my own family. No, I'm to have no hand in the diſpoſal of my own children. No, I'm nobody. I'm to be a mere article of family lumbe; a piece of crack'd china to be ſtuck up in a corner.

OLIVIA.

OLIVIA.

Dear Sir, nothing but the dread of your authority could induce us to conceal it from you.

CROAKER.

No, no, my consequence is no more; I'm as little minded as a dead Russian in winter, just stuck up with a pipe in his mouth till there comes a thaw—It goes to my heart to vex her. (*Aside.*)

OLIVIA.

I was prepar'd, Sir, for your anger, and despair'd of pardon, even while I presume to ask it. But your severity shall never abate my affection, as my punishment is but justice.

CROAKER.

And yet you should not despair neither, Livy. We ought to hope all for the best.

OLIVIA.

And do you permit me to hope, Sir? Can I ever expect to be forgiven? But hope has too long deceived me.

CROAKER.

Why then, child, it shan't deceive you now, for I forgive you this very moment. I forgive you all; and now you are indeed my daughter.

OLIVIA.

O transport! This kindness overpowers me.

CROAKER.

I was always against severity to our children. We have been young and giddy ourselves, and we can't expect boys and girls to be old before their time.

OLIVIA.

OLIVIA.

What generofity! But can you forget the many falſehoods, the diſſimulation——

CROAKER.

You did indeed diſſemble, you urchin you; but where's the girl that won't diſſemble for an huſband? My wife and I had never been married, if we had not diſſembled a little beforehand.

OLIVIA.

It ſhall be my future care never to put ſuch generofity to a ſecond trial. And as for the partner of my offence and folly, from his native honour, and the juſt ſenſe he has of his duty, I can anſwer for him that——

Enter LEONTINE.

LEONTINE.

Permit him thus to anſwer for himſelf. (*Kneeling*.) Thus, Sir, let me ſpeak my gratitude for this unmerited forgiveneſs. Yes, Sir, this even exceeds all your former tenderneſs : I now can boaſt the moſt indulgent of fathers. The life he gave, compared to this, was but a trifling bleſſing.

CROAKER.

And, good Sir, who ſent for you, with that fine tragedy face, and flouriſhing manner? I don't know what we have to do with your gratitude upon this occaſion.

LEONTINE.

How, Sir! Is it poſſible to be ſilent, when ſo much obliged! Would you refuſe me the pleaſure of being grateful! of adding my thanks to my Olivia's! of ſharing in the tranſports that you have thus occaſioned?

CROAKER.

Lord, Sir, we can be happy enough, without your coming in to make up the party. I don't know what's the matter with the boy all this day; he has got into ſuch a rhodomontade manner all this morning!

LEONTINE.

But, Sir, I that have ſo large a part in the benefit, is it not my duty to ſhew my joy? is the being admitted to your favour ſo ſlight an obligation? is the happineſs of marrying my Olivia ſo ſmall a bleſſing?

CROAKER.

Marrying Olivia! marrying Olivia! marrying his own ſiſter! Sure the boy is out of his ſenſes. His own ſiſter!

LEONTINE.

My ſiſter!

OLIVIA.

Siſter! How have I been miſtaken! [*Aſide.*

LEONTINE.

Some curs'd miſtake in all this I find. [*Aſide.*

CROAKER.

What does the booby mean? or has he any meaning? Eh, what do you mean, you blockhead you?

LEONTINE.

Mean, Sir—why, Sir—only when my ſiſter is to be married, that I have the pleaſure of marrying her, Sir, that is, of giving her away, Sir—I have made a point of it.

CROAKER.

O, is that all. Give her away. You have made a point of it. Then you had as good make a point of firſt giving away yourſelf, as I'm going to prepare the writings between you and Miſs Richland this very minute. What a fuſs is here about nothing! Why, what's the matter now? I thought I had made you at leaſt as happy as you could wiſh.

OLIVIA.

O! yes, Sir, very happy.

CROAKER.

Do you foreſee any thing, child? You look as if you did. I think if any thing was to be foreſeen, I have as ſharp a look out as another: and yet I foreſee nothing. [*Exit.*

LEONTINE, OLIVIA.

OLIVIA.

What can it mean?

LEONTINE.

He knows ſomething, and yet for my life I can't tell what.

OLIVIA.

OLIVIA.

It can't be the connection between us, I'm pretty certain.

LEONTINE.

Whatever it be, my dearest, I'm resolved to put it out of fortune's power to repeat our mortification. I'll haste and prepare for our journey to Scotland this very evening. My friend Honeywood has promised me his advice and assistance. I'll go to him, and repose our distresses on his friendly bosom: and I know so much of his honest heart, that if he can't relieve our uneasinesses, he will at least share them.

[*Exeunt.*

ACT THE THIRD.

SCENE, Young HONEYWOOD's Houſe.

BAILIFF, HONEYWOOD, FOLLOWER.

BAILIFF.

LOOKEY, Sir, I have arreſted as good men as you in my time: no diſparagement of you neither. Men that would go forty guineas on a game of cribbage. I challenge the town to ſhew a man in more genteeler practice than myſelf.

HONEYWOOD.

Without all queſtion, Mr. ——. I forget your name, Sir?

BAILIFF.

How can you forget what you never knew; he! he! he!

HONEYWOOD.

May I beg leave to aſk your name?

BAILIFF.

Yes, you may.

HONEYWOOD.

Then, pray, Sir, what is your name, Sir?

BAILIFF.

BAILIFF.

That I didn't promiſe to tell you. He! he! he! A joke breaks no bones, as we ſay among us that practiſe the law.

HONEYWOOD.

You may have reaſon for keeping it a ſecret, perhaps?

BAILIFF.

The law does nothing without reaſon. I'm aſham'd to tell my name to no man, Sir. If you can ſhew cauſe, as why, upon a ſpecial capus, that I ſhould prove my name—But, come, Timothy Twitch is my name. And, now you know my name, what have you to ſay to that?

HONEYWOOD.

Nothing in the world, good Mr. Twitch, but that I have a favour to aſk, that's all.

BAILIFF.

Ay, favours are more eaſily aſked than granted, as we ſay among us that practiſe the law. I have taken an oath againſt granting favours. Would you have me perjure myſelf?

HONEYWOOD.

But my requeſt will come recommended in ſo ſtrong a manner, as, I believe, you'll have no ſcruple (*pulling out his purſe*) The thing is only this: I believe I ſhall be able to diſcharge this trifle in two or three days at fartheſt; but as I would not have the affair known for the world, I have thoughts of keeping you, and your good friend here, about me till the debt is difcharged; for which I fhall be properly grateful.

BAILIFF.

Oh? that's another maxum, and altogether within my oath. For certain, if an honeft man is to get any thing by a thing, there's no reafon why all things fhould not be done in civility.

HONEYWOOD.

Doubtlefs, all trades muft live, Mr. Twitch; and yours is a neceffary one. (*Gives him money.*)

BAILIFF.

Oh! your honour; I hope your honour takes nothing amifs as I does, as I does nothing but my duty in fo doing. I'm fure no man can fay I ever give a gentleman, that was a gentleman, ill ufage. If I faw that a gentleman was a gentleman, I have taken money not to fee him for ten weeks together.

HONEYWOOD.

Tendernefs is a virtue, Mr. Twitch.

BAILIFF.

Ay, Sir, it's a perfect treafure. I love to fee a gentleman with a tender heart. I don't know, but I think I have a tender heart myfelf. If all that I have loft by my heart was put together, it would make a—but no matter for that.

HONEYWOOD.

Don't account it loft, Mr. Twitch. The ingratitude of the world can never deprive us of the con-

fcious

ſcious happineſs of having acted with humanity ourſelves.

BAILIFF.

Humanity, Sir, is a jewel. It's better than gold. I love humanity. People may ſay, that we, in our way, have no humanity; but I'll ſhew you my humanity this moment. There's my follower here, little Flanigan, with a wife and four children, a guinea or two would be more to him, than twice as much to another. Now, as I can't ſhew him any humanity myſelf, I muſt beg leave you'll do it for me.

HONEYWOOD.

I aſſure you, Mr. Twitch, yours is a moſt powerful recommendation. (*Giving money to the follower.*)

BAILIFF.

Sir, you're a gentleman. I ſee you know what to do with your money. But, to buſineſs: we are to be with you here as your friends, I ſuppoſe. But ſet in caſe company comes.—Little Flanigan here, to be ſure, has a good face; a very good face: but then, he is a little ſeedy, as we ſay among us that practiſe the law. Not well in cloaths. Smoke the pocket-holes.

HONEYWOOD.

Well, that ſhall be remedied without delay.

Enter SERVANT.

SERVANT.

Sir, Miſs Richland is below.

HONEYWOOD.

How unlucky! Detain her a moment. We muſt improve my good friend, little Mr. Flanigan's appearance firſt. Here, let Mr. Flanigan have a ſuit of my cloaths—quick—the brown and ſilver—Do you hear?

SERVANT.

That your honour gave away to the begging gentleman that makes verſes, becauſe it was as good as new.

HONEYWOOD.

The white and gold then,

SERVANT.

That, your honour, I made bold to ſell, becauſe it was good for nothing.

HONEYWOOD.

Well, the firſt that comes to hand then. The blue and gold then. I believe Mr. Flanigan will look beſt in blue. [*Exit* Flanigan.

BAILIFF.

Rabbit me, but little Flanigan will look well in any thing. Ah, if your honour knew that bit of fleſh as well as I do, you'd be perfectly in love with him. There's not a prettier ſcout in the four counties after a ſhy-cock than he: ſcents like a hound; ſticks like a weazle. He was maſter of the ceremonics nies to the black queen of Morocco, when I took him to follow me. (*Re-enter* Flanigan.) Heh, ecod, I think he looks ſo well, that I don't care if I have a ſuit from the ſame place for myſelf.

HONEYWOOD.

Well, well, I hear the lady coming. Dear Mr. Twitch, I beg you'll give your friend directions not to ſpeak. As for yourſelf, I know you will ſay nothing without being directed.

BAILIFF.

Never you fear me; I'll ſhew the lady that I have ſomething to ſay for myſelf as well as another. One man has one way of talking, and another man has another, that's all the difference between them.

Enter Miſs RICHLAND and her MAID.

Miſs RICHLAND.

You'll be ſurpriz'd, Sir, with this viſit. But you know I'm yet to thank you for chuſing my little library.

HONEYWOOD.

Thanks, madam, are unneceſſary; as it was I that was obliged by your commands. Chairs here. Two of my very good friends, Mr. Twitch and Mr. Flanigan. Pray, gentlemen, ſit without ceremony.

Miſs RICHLAND.

Who can theſe odd-looking men be! I fear it is as I was informed. It muſt be ſo. (*Aſide.*)

BAILIFF,

BAILIFF, after a Pauſe.

Pretty weather, very pretty weather for the time of the year, madam.

FOLLOWER.

Very good circuit weather in the country.

HONEYWOOD.

You officers are generally ſavourites among the ladies. My friends, madam, have been upon very diſagreeable duty, I aſſure you. The fair ſhould, in ſome meaſure, recompence the toils of the brave!

Miſs RICHLAND.

Our officers do indeed deſerve every favour. The gentlemen are in the marine ſervice, I preſume, Sir?

HONEYWOOD.

Why, madam, they do—occaſionally ſerve in the fleet, madam. A dangerous ſervice!

Miſs RICHLAND.

I'm told ſo. And I own, it has often ſurprized me, that while we have had ſo many inſtances of bravery there, we have had ſo few of wit at home to praiſe it.

HONEYWOOD.

I grant, madam, that our poets have not written as our ſoldiers have fought; but they have done all they could, and Hawke or Amherſt could do do more.

Miſs RICHLAND.

I'm quite diſpleaſed when I ſee a fine ſubject ſpoiled by a dull writer,

HONEY-

HONEYWOOD.

We ſhould not be ſo ſevere againſt dull writers, madam. It is ten to one, but the dulleſt writer exceeds the moſt rigid French critic who preſumes to deſpiſe him.

FOLLOWER.

Damn the French, the parle vous, and all that belongs to them.

Miſs RICHLAND.

Sir!

HONEYWOOD.

Ha, ha, ha! honeſt Mr. Flanigan. A true Engliſh officer, madam; he's not contented with beating the French, but he will ſcold them too.

Miſs RICHLAND.

Yet, Mr. Honeywood, this does not convince me but that ſeverity in criticiſm is neceſſary. It was our firſt adopting the ſeverity of French taſte, that has brought them in turn to taſte us,

BAILIFF.

Taſte us! By the Lord, madam, they devour us, Give monſeers but a taſte, and I'll be damn'd but they come in for a bellyful.

Miſs RICHLAND.

Very extraordinary this!

FOLLOWER.

But very true. What makes the bread riſing? the parle vous that devour us. What makes the mutton fivepence a pound? the parle vous that eat

it

it up. What makes the beer threepence-halfpenny a pot?——

HONEYWOOD.

Ah! the vulgar rogues; all will be out. (*Aside.*) Right, gentlemen, very right, upon my word, and quite to the purpofe. They draw a parallel, madam, between the mental tafte and that of our fenfes. We are injured as much by French feverity in the one, as by French rapacity in the other. That's their meaning.

Mifs RICHLAND.

Though I don't fee the force of the parallel, yet, I'll own, that we fhould fometimes pardon books, as we do our friends, that have now and then agreeable abfurdities to recommend them.

BAILIFF.

That's all my eye. The king only can pardon, as the laws fays: for, fet in cafe——

HONEYWOOD.

I'm quite of your opinion, Sir. I fee the whole drift of your argument. Yes, certainly, our prefuming to pardon any work, is arrogating a power that belongs to a another. If all have power to condemn, what writer can be free?

BAILIFF.

By his habus corpus. His habus corpus can fet him free at any time: for, fet in cafe——

HONEYWOOD.

I'm obliged to you, Sir, for the hint. If, madam, as my friend obferves, our laws are fo careful of of a gentleman's perſon, ſure we ought to be equally careful of his dearer part, his fame.

FOLLOWER.

Ay, but if ſo be a man's nabb'd, you know—

HONEYWOOD.

Mr. Flanigan, if you ſpoke for ever, you could not improve the laſt obſervation. For my own part, I think it concluſive.

BAILIFF.

As for the matter of that, mayhap—

HONEYWOOD.

Nay, Sir, give me leave in this inſtance to be poſitive. For, where is the neceſſity of cenſuring works without genius, which muſt ſhortly ſink of themſelves? what is it, but aiming our unneceſſary blow againſt a victim already under the hands of juſtice?

BAILIFF.

Juſtice! O, by the elevens, if you talk about juſtice, I think I am at home there: for, in a courſe of law—

HONEYWOOD.

My dear Mr. Twitch, I diſcern what you'd be at perfectly; and I believe the lady muſt be ſenſible of the art with which it is introduced. I ſuppoſe you perceive the meaning, madam of his courſe of law.

MIſs RICHLAND.

I proteſt, Sir, I do not. I perceive only that you anſwer one gentleman before he has finiſhed, and the other before he has well begun.

BAILIFF.

BAILIFF.

Madam, you are a gentlewoman, and I will make the matter out. This here queſtion is about ſeverity and juſtice, and pardon, and the like of they. Now to explain the thing—

HONEYWOOD.

O! curſe your explanations. [*Aſide.*

Enter SERVANT.

SERVANT.

Mr. Leontine, Sir, below, deſires to ſpeak with you upon earneſt buſineſs.

HONEYWOOD.

That's lucky. (*Aſide.*) Dear madam, you'll excuſe me and my good friends here, for a few minutes. There are books, madam, to amuſe you. Come, gentlemen, you know I make no ceremony with ſuch friends. After you, Sir. Excuſe me. Well, if I muſt. But I know your natural politeneſs.

BAILIFF.

Before and behind, you know.

FOLLOWER.

Ay, ay, before and behind, before and behind.

[*Exeunt* Honeywood, Bailiff, *and* Follower.

Miſs RICHLAND.

What can all this mean, Garnet?

GARNET.

Mean, madam! why, what ſhould it mean, but what Mr. Lofty ſent you here to ſee! Theſe people

ple he calls officers are officers ſure enough: ſheriff's officers; bailiffs, madam.

Miſs RICHLAND.

Ay, it is certainly ſo. Well, though his perplexities are far from giving me pleaſure, yet I own there's ſomething very ridiculous in them, and a juſt puniſhment for his diſſimulation.

GARNET.

And ſo they are. But I wonder, madam, that the lawyer you juſt employed to pay his debts, and ſet him free, has not done it by this time. He ought at leaſt to have been here before now. But lawyers are always more ready to get a man into troubles, than out of them.

Enter Sir WILLIAM.

Sir WILLIAM.

For Miſs Richland to undertake ſetting him free, I own, was quite unexpected. It has totally unhinged my ſchemes to reclaim him. Yet, it gives me pleaſure to find, that, among a number of worthleſs friendſhips, he has made one acquiſition of real value; for there muſt be ſome ſofter paſſion on her ſide that prompts this generoſity. Ha! here before me: I'll endeavour to ſound her affections. Madam, as I am the perſon that have had ſome demands upon the gentleman of this houſe, I hope you'll excuſe me, if, before I enlarged him, I wanted to ſee yourſelf.

Miſs

Miſs RICHLAND.

The precaution was very unneceſſary, Sir. I ſuppoſe your wants were only ſuch as my agent had power to ſatisfy.

Sir WILLIAM.

Partly, madam. But, I was alſo willing you ſhould be fully apprized of the character of the gentleman you intended to ſerve.

Miſs RICHLAND.

It muſt come, ſir, with a very ill grace from you. To cenſure it, after what you have done, would look like malice; and, to ſpeak favourably of a character you have oppreſſed, would be impeaching your own. And ſure, his tenderneſs, his humanity, his univerſal friendſhip, may atone for many faults.

Sir WILLIAM.

That friendſhip, madam, which is exerted in too wide a ſphere, becomes totally uſeleſs. Our bounty, like a drop of water, diſappears when diffuſed too widely. They, who pretend moſt to this univerſal benevolence, are either deceivers, or dupes. Men who deſire to cover their private ill-nature, by a pretended regard for all; or, men who, reaſoning themſelves into falſe feelings, are more earneſt in purſuit of ſplendid, than of uſeful virtues.

Miſs RICHLAND.

I am ſurpriſed, Sir, to hear one, who has probably been a gainer by the folly of others, ſo ſevere in his cenſure of it.

Sir

Sir WILLIAM.

Whatever I may have gained by folly, madam, you ſee I am willing to prevent your loſing by it.

Miſs RICHLAND.

You cares for me, Sir, are unneceſſary. I always ſuſpect thoſe ſervices which are denied where they are wanted, and offered, perhaps, in hopes of a refuſal. No, Sir, my directions have been given, and I inſiſt upon their being complied with.

Sir WILLIAM.

Thou amiable woman! I can no longer contain the expreſſions of my gratitude: my pleaſure. You ſee before you one, who has been equally careful of his intereſt; one, who has for ſome time been a concealed ſpectator of his follies, and only puniſhed, in hopes to reclaim them—his uncle!

Miſs RICHLAND.

Sir William Honeywood! You amaze me. How ſhall I conceal my confuſion? I fear, Sir, you'll think I have been too forward in my ſervices. I confeſs I—

Sir WILLIAM.

Don't make any apologies, madam. I only find myſelf unable to repay the obligation. And yet, I have been trying my intereſt of late to ſerve you. Having learnt, madam, that you had ſome demands upon government, I have, though unaſked, been your ſolicitor there.

Miſs RICHLAND.

Sir, I'm infinitely obliged to your intentions. But my guardian has employed another gentleman who aſſures him of ſucceſs.

Sir WILLIAM.

Who, the important little man that viſits here? Truſt me, madam, he's quite contemptible among men in power, and utterly unable to ſerve you. Mr. Lofty's promiſes are much better known to people of faſhion, than his perſon, I aſſure you.

Miſs RICHLAND.

How have we been deceived! As ſure as can be, here he comes.

Sir WILLIAM.

Does he! Remember I'm to continue unknown. My return to England has not as yet been made public. With what impudence he enters!

Enter LOFTY.

LOFTY.

Let the chariot—let my chariot drive off; I'll viſit to his grace's in a chair. Miſs Richland here before me! Punctual, as uſual, to the calls of humanity. I'm very ſorry, madam, things of this kind ſhould happen, eſpecially to a man I have ſhewn every where, and carried amongſt us as a particular acquaintance.

Miſs RICHLAND.

I find, Sir, you have the art of making the misfortunes of others your own.

LOFTY.

LOFTY.

My dear madam, what can a private man like me do? One man can't do every thing; and then, I do ſo much in this way every day: let me ſee; ſomething conſiderable might be done for him by ſubſcription; it could not fail if I carried the liſt. I'll undertake to ſet down a brace of dukes, two dozen lords, and half the lower houſe, at my own peril.

Sir WILLIAM.

And, after all, it's more than probable, Sir, he might reject the offer of ſuch powerful patronage.

LOFTY.

Then, madam, what can we do? You know I never make promiſes. In truth, I once or twice tried to do ſomething with him in the way of buſineſs; but, as I often told his uncle, Sir William Honeywood, the man was utterly impracticable.

Sir WILLIAM.

His uncle! Then that gentleman, I ſuppoſe, is a particular friend of yours.

LOFTY.

Meaning me, Sir?—Yes, madam, as I often ſaid, my dear Sir William, you are ſenſible I would do any thing, as far as my poor intereſt goes, to ſerve your family: but what can be done? there's no procuring firſt-rate places for ninth-rate abilities.

MIſs RICHLAND.

I have heard of Sir William Honeywood; he's abroad in employment: he confided in your judgment, I ſuppoſe.

LOFTY.

Why, yes, madam, I believe Sir William had ſome reaſon to confide in my Judgment; one little reaſon, perhaps.

MIſs RICHLAND.

Pray, Sir, What was it?

LOFTY.

Why, madam—but let it go no further—it was I procured him his place.

Sir WILLIAM.

Did you, Sir?

LOFTY.

Either you or I, Sir,

MIſs RICHLAND.

This, Mr. Lofty, was very kind indeed.

LOFTY.

I did love him, to be ſure; he had ſome amuſing qualities; no man was fitter to be toaſt-maſter to a club, or had a better head.

MIſs RICHLAND.

A better head?

LOFTY.

Ay, at a bottle. To be ſure, he was as dull as a choice ſpirit: but hang it, he was grateful, very grateful; and gratitude hides a multitude of faults.

Sir

Sir WILLIAM.

He might have reaſon, perhaps. His place is pretty conſiderable, I'm told.

LOFTY.

A trifle, a mere trifle, among us men of buſineſs. The truth is, he wanted dignity to fill up a greater.

Sir WILLIAM.

Dignity of perſon, do you mean, Sir? I'm told he's much about my ſize and figure, Sir.

LOFTY.

Ay, tall enough for a marching regiment; but then he wanted a ſomething—a conſequence of form—a kind of a—I believe the lady perceives my meaning.

Miſs RICHLAND.

O, perfectly: you courtiers can do any thing, I ſee.

LOFTY.

My dear madam, all this is but a meer exchange: we do greater things for one another every day. Why, as thus, now: let me ſuppoſe you the firſt lord of the treaſury; you have an employment in you that I want; I have a place in me that you want! do me here, do you there: intereſt of both ſides, few words, flat, done and done, and its over.

Sir WILLIAM.

A thought ſtrikes me. (*Aſide.*) Now you mention Sir William Honeywood, madam; and as he ſeems, Sir, an acquaintance of yours; you'll be glad to hear he's arrived from Italy; I had it from a friend who knows him as well as he does me, and you may depend on my information.

LOFTY.

The devil he is! If I had known that, we ſhould not have been quite ſo well acquainted. (*Aſide.*)

Sir WILLIAM.

He is certainly return'd; and, as this gentleman is a friend of yours, he can be of ſignal ſervice to us, by introducing me to him; there are ſome papers relative to your affairs, that require diſpatch and his inſpection.

Miſs RICHLAND.

This gentleman, Mr. Lofty, is a perſon employed in my affairs: I know you'll ſerve us.

LOFTY.

My dear madam, I live but to ſerve you. Sir William ſhall even wait upon him, if you think proper to command it.

Sir WILLIAM.

That would be quite unneceſſary.

LOFTY.

Well, we muſt introduce you then. Call upon me—let me ſee—ay, in two days.

Sir WILLIAM.

Now, or the opportunity will be loſt for ever.

LOFTY.

Well, if it muſt be now, now let it be. But damn it, that's unfortunate; my lord Grig's curſed Pen-

ſacola

ſacola buſineſs comes on this very hour, and I'm engaged to attend—another time—

Sir WILLIAM.

A ſhort letter to Sir William will do.

LOFTY.

You ſhall have it; yet, in my opinion, a letter is a very bad way of going to work; face to face, that's my way.

Sir WILLIAM.

The letter, Sir, will do quite as well.

LOFTY.

Zounds! Sir, do you pretend to direct me; direct me in the buſineſs of office? Do you know me, Sir? who am I?

Miſs RICHLAND.

Dear Mr. Lofty, this requeſt is not ſo much his as mine; if my commands—but you deſpiſe my power.

LOFTY.

Delicate creature! your commands could even controul a debate at midnight: to a power ſo conſtitutional, I am all obedience and tranquillity. He ſhall have a letter; where is my ſecretary! Dubardieu! And yet, I proteſt I don't like this way of doing buſineſs. I think if I ſpoke firſt to Sir William—But you will have it ſo.

[*Exit with Miſs* Richland.

Sir WILLIAM, alone.

Ha, ha, ha! This too is one of my nephew's hopeful aſſociates. O vanity, thou conſtant deceiver, how do all thy efforts to exalt, ſerve but to ſink us! Thy falſe colourings, like thoſe employed, to heighten beauty, only ſeem to mend that bloom which they contribute to deſtroy. I'm not diſpleaſed at this interview: expoſing this fellow's impudence to the contempt it deſerves, may be of uſe to my deſign; at leaſt, if he can reflect, it will be of uſe to himſelf.

Enter JARVIS.

Sir WILLIAM.

How now, Jarvis, where's your maſter, my nephew?

JARVIS.

At his wit's end, I believe: he's ſcarce gotten out of one ſcrape, but he's running his head into another.

Sir WILLIAM.

How ſo?

JARVIS.

The houſe has but juſt been cleared of the bailiffs, and now he's again engaging tooth and nail in aſſiſting old Croaker's ſon to patch up a clandeſtine match with the young lady that paſſes in the houſe for his ſiſter.

Sir WILLIAM.

Ever buſy to ſerve others.

JARVIS.

JARVIS.

Aye, any body but himſelf. The young couple, it ſeems, are juſt ſetting out for Scotland; and he ſupplies them with money for the journey.

Sir WILLIAM.

Money! how is he able to ſupply others, who has ſcarce any for himſelf?

JARVIS.

Why, there it is: he has no money, that's true; but then, as he never ſaid no to any requeſt in his life, he has given them a bill, drawn by a friend of his upon a merchant in the city, which I am to get changed; for you muſt know that I am to go with them to Scotland myſelf.

Sir WILLIAM.

How!

JARVIS.

It ſeems the young gentleman is obliged to take a different road from his miſtreſs, as he is to call upon an uncle of his that lives out of the way, in order to prepare a place for their reception, when they return; ſo they have borrowed me from my maſter, as the propereſt perſon to attend the young lady down.

Sir WILLIAM.

To the land of matrimony! A pleaſant journey, Jarvis.

JARVIS.

Ay, but I'm only to have all the fatigues on't.

Sir

Sir WILLIAM.

Well, it may be ſhorter, and leſs fatiguing, than you imagine. I know but too much of the young lady's family and connections, whom I have ſeen abroad. I have alſo diſcovered that Miſs Richland is not indifferent to my thoughtleſs nephew; and will endeavour, though I fear, in vain, to eſtabliſh that connection. But, come, the letter I wait for muſt be almoſt finiſhed; I'll let you further into my intentions, in the next room. [*Exeunt.*

ACT

ACT THE FOURTH.

SCENE, CROAKER's House.

LOFTY.

WELL, fure the devil's in me of late, for running my head into fuch defiles, as nothing but a genius like my own could draw me from. I was formerly contented to hufband out my places and penfions with fome degree of frugality; but, curfe it, of late I have given away the whole Court Regifter in lefs time than they could print the title page: yet, hang it, why fcruple a lie or two to come at a fine girl, when I every day tell a thoufand for nothing. Ha! Honeywood here before me. Could Mifs Richland have fet him at liberty?

Enter HONEYWOOD.

Mr. Honeywood, I'm glad to fee you abroad again. I find my concurrence was not neceffary in your unfortunate affairs. I had put things in a train to do your bufinefs; but it is not for me to fay what I intended doing.

Ho-

HONEYWOOD.

It was unfortunate indeed, Sir. But what adds to my uneaſineſs is, that while you ſeem to be acquainted with my misfortune, I, myſelf, continue ſtill a ſtranger to my benefactor.

LOFTY.

How! not know the friend that ſerved you?

HONEYWOOD.

Can't gueſs at the perſon.

LOFTY.

Inquire.

HONEYWOOD.

I have; but all I can learn is, that he chuſes to remain concealed, and that all inquiry muſt be fruitleſs.

LOFTY.

Muſt be fruitleſs?

HONEYWOOD.

Abſolutely fruitleſs.

LOFTY.

Sure of that?

HONEYWOOD.

Very ſure.

LOFTY.

Then I'll be damn'd if you ſhall ever know it from me.

HONEYWOOD.

How, Sir!

LOFTY.

I ſuppoſe now, Mr. Honeywood, you think my rent-roll very conſiderable, and that I have vaſt ſums of money to throw away; I know you do. The world to be ſure ſays ſuch things of me.

HONEYWOOD.

The world, by what I learn, is no ſtranger to your generoſity. But where does this tend?

LOFTY.

To nothing; nothing in the world. The town, to be ſure, when it makes ſuch a thing as me the ſubject of converſation, has aſſerted, that I never yet patronized a man of merit.

HONEYWOOD.

I have heard inſtances to the contrary, even from yourſelf.

LOFTY.

Yes, Honeywood, and there are inſtances to the contrary, that you ſhall never hear from myſelf.

HONEYWOOD.

Ha! dear Sir, permit me to aſk you but one queſtion.

LOFTY.

Sir, aſk me no queſtions: I ſay, Sir, aſk me no queſtions; I'll be damn'd, if I anſwer them.

HONEYWOOD.

I will aſk no further. My friend! my benefactor, it is, it muſt be here, that I am indebted for freedom, for honour. Yes, thou worthieſt of men,

from

from the beginning I ſuſpected it, but was afraid to return thanks; which, if undeſerved, might ſeem reproaches.

LOFTY.

I proteſt I don't underſtand all this, Mr. Honeywood. You treat me very cavalierly. I do aſſure you, Sir.—Blood, Sir, can't a man be permitted to enjoy the luxury of his own feelings, without all this parade?

HONEYWOOD.

Nay, do not attempt to conceal an action that adds to your honour. Your looks, your air, your manner, all confeſs it.

LOFTY.

Confeſs it, Sir! Torture itſelf, Sir, ſhall never bring me to confeſs it. Mr. Honeywood, I have admitted you upon terms of friendſhip. Don't let us fall out; make me happy, and let this be buried in oblivion. You know I hate oſtentation; you know I do. Come, come, Honeywood, you know I always loved to be a friend, and not a patron. I beg this may make no kind of diſtance between us. Come, come, you and I muſt be more familiar—Indeed we muſt.

HONEYWOOD.

Heavens! Can I ever repay ſuch friendſhip! Is there any way! Thou beſt of men, can I ever return the obligation?

LOFTY.

LOFTY.

A bagatelle, a mere bagatelle! But I ſee your heart is labouring to be grateful. You ſhall be grateful. It would be cruel to diſappoint you.

HONEYWOOD.

How! teach me the manner. Is there any way?

LOFTY.

From this moment you're mine. Yes, my friend, you ſhall know it—I'm in love.

HONEYWOOD.

And can I aſſiſt you?

LOFTY.

Nobody ſo well.

HONEYWOOD.

In what manner. I'm all impatience.

LOFTY.

You ſhall make love for me.

HONEYWOOD.

And to whom ſhall I ſpeak in your favour?

LOFTY.

To a lady with whom you have great intereſt, I aſſure you: Miſs Richland.

HONEYWOOD.

Miſs Richland!

LOFTY.

Yes, Miſs Richland. She has ſtruck the blow up to the hilt in my boſom, by Jupiter.

Ho-

HONEYWOOD.

Heavens! was ever any thing more unfortunate! It is too much to be endured.

LOFTY.

Unfortunate indeed! And yet I can endure it, till you have opened the affair to her for me. Between ourſelves, I think ſhe likes me. I'm not apt to boaſt, but I think ſhe does.

HONEYWOOD.

Indeed! But, do you know the perſon you apply to?

LOFTY.

Yes, I know you are her friend and mine: that's enough. To you, therefore, I commit the ſucceſs of my paſſion. I'll ſay no more, let friendſhip do the reſt. I have only to add, that if at any time my little intereſt can be of ſervice—but, hang it, I'll make no promiſes—you know my intereſt is yours at any time. No apologies, my friend, I'll not be anſwered, it ſhall be ſo. [*Exit.*

HONEYWOOD.

Open, generous, unſuſpecting man! He little thinks that I love her too; and with ſuch an ardent paſſion!—But then it was ever but a vain and hopeleſs one; my torment, my perſecution! What ſhall I do! Love, friendſhip, an hopeleſs paſſion, a deſerving friend! Love, that has been my tormentor; a friend, that has, perhaps, diſtreſſed himſelf, to ſerve me. It ſhall be ſo. Yes, I will diſcard the fondling hope from my boſom, and exert all my influence

influence in his favour. And yet to see her in the possession of another!—Insupportable! But then to betray a generous, trusting friend!—Worse, worse! Yes, I'm resolved. Let me but be the instrument of their happiness, and then quit a country, where I must for ever despair of finding my own. [*Exit.*

Enter OLIVIA, and GARNET, who carries a Milliner's Box.

OLIVIA.

Dear me, I wish this journey were over. No news of Jarvis yet? I believe the old peevish creature delays purely to vex me.

GARNET.

Why, to be sure, madam, I did hear him say, a little snubbing, before marriage, would teach you to bear it the better afterwards.

OLIVIA.

To be gone a full hour, though he had only to get a bill changed in the city! How provoking!

GARNET.

I'll lay my life, Mr. Leontine, that had twice as much to do, is setting off by this time from his inn; and here you are left behind.

OLIVIA.

Well, let us be prepared for his coming, however. Are you sure you have omitted nothing, Garnet?

GARNET.

Not a ſtick, madam—all's here. Yet I wiſh you could take the white and ſilver to be married in. It's the worſt luck in the world, in any thing but white. I knew one Bett Stubbs, of our town, that was married in red; and, as ſure as eggs is eggs, the bridegroom and ſhe had a miff before morning.

OLIVIA.

No matter. I'm all impatience till we are out of the houſe.

GARNET.

Bleſs me, madam, I had almoſt forgot the wedding-ring!—The ſweet little thing—I don't think it would go on my little finger. And what if I put in a gentleman's night-cap, in caſe of neceſſity, madam? But here's Jarvis.

Enter JARVIS.

OLIVIA.

O, Jarvis, are you come at laſt? We have been ready this half hour. Now let's be going. Let us fly!

JARVIS.

Aye, to Jericho; for we ſhall have no going to Scotland this bout, I fancy.

OLIVIA.

How! What's the matter?

JARVIS.

Money, money, is the matter, madam. We have got no money. What the plague do you ſend me of of your fool's errand for? My maſter's bill upon the city is not worth a ruſh. Here it is; Mrs. Garnet may pin up her hair with it.

OLIVIA.

Undone! How could Honeywood ſerve us ſo! What ſhall we do? Can't we go without it?

JARVIS.

Go to Scotland without money! To Scotland without money! Lord how ſome people underſtand geography! We might as well ſet ſail for Patagonia upon a cork jacket.

OLIVIA.

Such a diſappointment! What a baſe inſincere man was your maſter, to ſerve us in this manner? Is this his good nature?

JARVIS.

Nay, don't talk ill of my maſter, madam. I won't bear to hear any body talk ill of him but myſelf.

GARNET.

Bleſs us! now I think on't, madam, you need not be under any uneaſineſs: I ſaw Mr. Leontine receive forty guineas from his father juſt before he ſet out, and he can't yet have left the inn. A ſhort letter will reach him there.

OLIVIA.

Well remember'd, Garnet; I'll write immediately. How's this! Bleſs me, my hand trembles ſo, I can't write a word. Do you write, Garnet; and, upon ſecond thought, it will be better from you.

GARNET.

Truly, madam, I write and indite but poorly. I never was kute at my larning. But I'll do what I can to pleaſe you. Let me ſee. All out of my own head, I ſuppoſe?

OLIVIA.

Whatever you pleaſe.

GARNET.

(*Writing.*) Muſter Croaker—Twenty guineas, madam?

OLIVIA.

Aye, twenty will do.

GARNET.

At the bar of the Talbot till call'd for. Expedition—Will be blown up—All of a ſlame—Quick diſpatch—Cupid, the little god of love—I conclude it, madam, with Cupid; I love to ſee a love-letter end like poetry.

OLIVIA.

Well, well, what you pleaſe, any thing. But how ſhall we ſend it? I can truſt none of the ſervants of this family.

GARNET.

Odſo, madam, Mr. Honeywood's butler is in the next room: he's a dear, ſweet man; he'll do any thing for me.

JARVIS.

He! the dog, he'll certainly commit ſome blunder. He's drunk and ſober ten times a day.

OLIVIA.

OLIVIA.

No matter. Fly, Garnet: any body we can truſt will do. [*Exit* Garnet.] Well, Jarvis, now we can have nothing more to interrupt us. You may take up the things, and carry them on to the inn. Have you no hands, Jarvis?

JARVIS.

Soft and fair, young lady. You, that are going to be married, think things can never be done too faſt: but, we, that are old, and know what we are about, muſt elope methodically, madam.

OLIVIA.

Well, ſure, if my indiſcretions were to be done over again——

JARVIS.

My life for it, you would do them ten times over.

OLIVIA.

Why will you talk ſo? If you knew how unhappy they make me——

JARVIS.

Very unhappy, no doubt: I was once juſt as unhappy when I was going to be married myſelf. I'll tell you a ſtory about that——

OLIVIA.

A ſtory! when I'm all impatience to be away. Was there ever ſuch a dilatory creature!——

JARVIS.

Well, madam, if we muſt march, why we will march; that's all. Though, odds bobs, we have ſtill forgot one thing we ſhould never travel without—a caſe of good razors, and a box of ſhaving-powder. But no matter, I believe we ſhall be pretty well ſhaved by the way. [*Going.*

Enter GARNET.

GARNET.

Undone, undone, madam. Ah, Mr. Jarvis, you ſaid right enough. As ſure as death Mr. Honeywood's rogue of a drunken butler, dropp'd the letter before he went ten yards from the door. There's old Croaker has juſt pick'd it up, and is this moment reading it to himſelf in the hall.

OLIVIA.

Unfortunate! We ſhall be diſcovered.

GARNET.

No, madam: don't be uneaſy, he can make neither head nor tail of it. To be ſure he looks as if he was broke looſe from Bedlam about it, but he can't find what it means for all that. O lud, he is coming this way all in the horrors!

OLIVIA.

Then let us leave the houſe this inſtant, for fear he ſhould aſk farther queſtions. In the mean time, Garnet, do you write and ſend off juſt ſuch another, [*Exeunt.*

Enter

Enter CROAKER.

CROAKER.

Death and deſtruction! Are all the horrors of air, fire and water to be levelled only at me! Am I only to be ſingled out for gunpowder-plots, combuſtibles and conflagration! Here it is—An incendiary letter dropped at my door. "To muſter Croaker, theſe, "with ſpeed." Aye, aye, plain enough the direction: all in the genuine incendiary ſpelling, and as cramp as the devil. "With ſpeed." O, confound your ſpeed. But let me read it once more. (*Reads.*) "Muſter Croaker as ſone as yoew ſee this "leve twenty guineas at the bar of the Talboot tell "called for or yowe and yower experetion will be "al blown up." Ah, but too plain. Blood and gunpowder in every line of it. Blown up! murderous dog! All blown up! Heavens! what have I and my poor family done, to be all blown up! (*Reads.*) "Our pockets are low, and money we muſt "have." Aye, there's the reaſon; they'll blow us up, becauſe they have got low pockets. (*Reads.*) "It is but a ſhort time you have to conſider; for if "this takes wind, the houſe will quickly be all of "a flame." Inhuman monſters! blow us up, and then burn us. The earthquake at Liſbon was but a bonfire to it. (*Reads.*) "Make quick diſpatch, "and ſo no more at preſent. But may Cupid, the "little god of love, go with you wherever you go" The little god of love! Cupid, the little god of love go with me! Go you to the devil, you and your little Cupid together; I'm fo frightened, I fcarce know whether I fit, ftand, or go. Perhaps this moment I'm treading on lighted matches, blazing brimftone and barrels of gunpowder. They are preparing to blow me up into the clouds. Murder! We fhall be all burnt in our beds; we fhall be all burnt in our beds.

Enter Mifs RICHLAND.

Mifs RICHLAND.

Lord, Sir, what's the matter?

CROAKER.

Murder's the matter. We fhall be all blown up in our beds before morning.

Mifs RICHLAND.

I hope not, Sir.

CROAKER.

What fignifies what you hope, madam, when I have a certificate of it here in my hand? Will nothing alarm my family? Sleeping and eating, fleeping and eating is the only work from morning till night in my houfe. My infenfible crew could fleep, though rock'd by an earthquake; and fry beef fteaks at a volcano.

Mifs RICHLAND.

But, Sir, you have alarmed them fo often already, we have nothing but earthquakes, famines, plagues and mad dogs from year's end to year's end. You remem-

remember, Sir, it is not above a month ago, you aſſured us of a conſpiracy among the bakers, to poiſon us in our bread; and ſo kept the whole family a week upon potatoes.

CROAKER.

And potatoes were too good for them. But why do I ſtand talking here with a girl, when I ſhould be facing the enemy without? Here, John, Nicodemus, ſearch the houſe. Look into the cellars, to ſee if there be any combuſtibles below; and above, in the apartments, that no matches be thrown in at the windows. Let all the fires be put out, and let the engine be drawn out in the yard, to play upon the houſe in caſe of neceſſity. [*Exit.*

Miſs RICHLAND, alone.

What can he mean by all this? Yet, why ſhould I inquire, when he alarms us in this manner almoſt every day! But Honeywood has deſired an interview with me in private. What can he mean? or, rather, what means this palpitation at his approach? It is the firſt time he ever ſhewed any thing in his conduct that ſeemed particular. Sure he cannot mean to——but he's here.

Enter HONEYWOOD.

HONEYWOOD.

I preſumed to ſolicit this interview, madam, before I left town, to be permitted——

Miſs

Miſs RICHLAND.

Indeed! Leaving town, Sir?—

HONEYWOOD.

Yes, madam; perhaps the kingdom. I have preſumed, I ſay, to deſire the favour of this interview, —in order to diſcloſe ſomething which our long friendſhip prompts. And yet my fears—

Miſs RICHLAND.

His fears! What are his fears to mine? (*Aſide.*) We have indeed been long acquainted, Sir; very long. If I remember, our firſt meeting was at the French ambaſſador's.—Do you recollect how you were pleaſed to rally me upon my complexion there?

HONEYWOOD.

Perfectly, madam: I preſumed to reprove you for painting: but your warmer bluſhes ſoon convinced the company, that the colouring was all from nature.

Miſs RICHLAND.

And yet you only meant it, in your good-natured way, to make me pay a compliment to myſelf. In the ſame manner you danced that night with the moſt aukward woman in company, becauſe you ſaw nobody elſe would take her out.

HONEYWOOD.

Yes; and was rewarded the next night, by dancing with the fineſt woman in company, whom every body wiſhed to take out.

Miſs

Miſs RICHLAND.

Well, Sir, if you thought ſo then, I fear your judgment has ſince corrected the errors of a firſt impreſſion. We generally ſhew to moſt advantage at firſt. Our ſex are like poor tradeſmen, that put all their beſt goods to be ſeen at the windows.

HONEYWOOD.

The firſt impreſſion, madam, did indeed deceive me. I expected to find a woman with all the faults of conſcious flattered beauty. I expected to find her vain and inſolent. But every day has ſince taught me that it is poſſible to poſſeſs ſenſe without pride, and beauty without affectation.

Miſs RICHLAND.

This, Sir, is a ſtyle very unuſual with Mr. Honeywood; and I ſhould be glad to know why he thus attempts to encreaſe that vanity, which his own leſſons have taught me to deſpiſe.

HONEYWOOD.

I aſk pardon, madam. Yet, from our long friendſhip, I preſumed I might have ſome right to offer, without offence, what you may refuſe without offending.

Miſs RICHLAND.

Sir! I beg you'd reflect; though, I fear, I ſhall ſcarce have any power to refuſe a requeſt of yours; yet you may be precipitate: conſider, Sir.

HONEYWOOD.

I own my raſhneſs; but, as I plead the cauſe of friendſhip, of one who loves—Don't be alarmed,

madam—

madam—who loves you with the moſt ardent paſſion, whoſe whole happineſs is placed in you—

Miſs RICHLAND.

I fear, Sir, I ſhall never find whom you mean, by this deſcription of him.

HONEYWOOD.

Ah, madam, it but too plainly points him out; though he ſhould be too humble himſelf to urge his pretenſions, or you too modeſt to underſtand them.

Miſs RICHLAND.

Well; it would be affectation any longer to pretend ignorance; and I will own, Sir, I have long been prejudiced in his favour. It was but natural to wiſh to make his heart mine, as he ſeemed himſelf ignorant of its value.

HONEYWOOD.

I ſee ſhe always loved him. (*Aſide.*) I find, madam, you're already ſenſible of his worth, his paſſion. How happy is my friend, to be the favourite of one with ſuch ſenſe to diſtinguiſh merit, and ſuch beauty to reward it.

Miſs RICHLAND.

Your friend, Sir! What friend?

HONEYWOOD.

My beſt friend—my friend Mr. Lofty, madam.

Miſs RICHLAND.

He, Sir!

HONEYWOOD.

Yes, he, madam. He is, indeed, what your warmeſt wiſhes might have formed him. And to his

his other qualities, he adds that of the moſt paſſionate regard for you.

Miſs RICHLAND.

Amazement!—No more of this, I beg you, Sir.

HONEYWOOD.

I ſee your confuſion, madam, and know how to interpret it. And, ſince I ſo plainly read the language of your heart, ſhall I make my friend happy, by communicating your ſentiments?

Miſs RICHLAND.

By no means.

HONEYWOOD.

Excuſe me; I muſt; I know you deſire it.

Miſs RICHLAND.

Mr. Honeywood, let me tell you, that you wrong my ſentiments and yourſelf. When I firſt applied to your friendſhip, I expected advice and aſſiſtance; but, now, Sir, I ſee that it is vain to expect happineſs from him, who has been ſo bad an œconomiſt of his own; and that I muſt diſclaim his friendſhip, who ceaſes to be a friend to himſelf. [*Exit.*

HONEYWOOD.

How is this! ſhe has confeſſed ſhe loved him, and yet ſhe ſeemed to part in diſpleaſure. Can I have done any thing to reproach myſelf with? No: I believe not: yet, after all, theſe things ſhould not be done by a third perſon; I ſhould have ſpared her confuſion. My friendſhip carried me a little too far.

Enter

Enter CROAKER, with the Letter in his Hand, and Mrs. CROAKER.

Mrs. CROAKER.

Ha! ha! ha! And ſo, my dear, it's your ſupreme wiſh that I ſhould be quite wretched upon this occaſion? ha! ha!

CROAKER, mimicking.

Ha! ha! ha! And ſo, my dear, it's your ſupreme pleaſure to give me no better conſolation?

Mrs. CROAKER.

Poſitively, my dear; what is this incendiary ſtuff and trumpery to me? our houſe may travel through the air like the houſe of Loretto, for aught I care, if I'm to be miſerable in it.

CROAKER.

Would to heaven it were converted into an houſe of correction for your benefit. Have we not every thing to alarm us? Perhaps, this very moment the tragedy is beginning.

Mrs. CROAKER.

Then let us reſerve our diſtreſs till the riſing of the curtain, or give them the money they want, and have done with them.

CROAKER.

Give them my money!—And pray, what right have they to my money?

Mrs. CROAKER.

And pray, what right then have you to my good humour?

CROAKER.

CROAKER.

And ſo your good humour adviſes me to part with my money? Why then, to tell your good humour a piece of my mind, I'd ſooner part with my wife. Here's Mr. Honeywood, ſee what he'll ſay to it. My dear Honeywood, look at this incendiary letter dropped at my door. It will freeze you with terror; and yet lovey here can read it—can read it, and laugh.

Mrs. CROAKER.

Yes, and ſo will Mr. Honeywood.

CROAKER.

If he does, I'll ſuffer to be hanged the next minute in the rogue's place, that's all.

Mrs. CROAKER.

Speak, Mr. Honeywood; is there any thing more fooliſh than my huſband's fright upon this occaſion?

HONEYWOOD.

It would not become me to decide, madam; but doubtleſs, the greatneſs of his terrors, now, will but invite them to renew their villainy another time.

Mrs. CROAKER.

I told you, he'd be of my opinion.

CROAKER.

How, Sir! do you maintain that I ſhould lie down under ſuch an injury, and ſhew, neither by my tears, or complaints, that I have ſomething of the ſpirit of a man in me?

Ho-

HONEYWOOD.

Pardon me, Sir. You ought to make the loudeſt complaints, if you deſire redreſs. The ſureſt way to have redreſs, is to be earneſt in the purſuit of it.

CROAKER.

Aye, whoſe opinion is he of now?

Mrs. CROAKER.

But don't you think that laughing off our fears is the beſt way!

HONEYWOOD.

What is the beſt, madam, few can ſay? but I'll maintain it to be a very wiſe way.

CROAKER.

But we're talking of the beſt. Surely the beſt way is to face the enemy in the field, and not wait till he plunders us in our very bed-chamber.

HONEYWOOD.

Why, Sir, as to the beſt, that—that's a very wiſe way too.

Mrs. CROAKER.

But can any thing be more abſurd, than to double our diſtreſſes by our apprehenſions, and put it in the power of every low fellow, that can ſcrawl ten words of wretched ſpelling, to torment us?

HONEYWOOD.

Without doubt, nothing more abſurd.

CROAKER.

How! would it not be more abſurd to deſpiſe the rattle till we are bit by the ſnake?

Ho-

HONEYWOOD.

Without doubt, perfectly abſurd.

CROAKER.

Then you are of my opinion?

HONEYWOOD.

Entirely.

Mrs. CROAKER.

And you reject mine?

HONEYWOOD.

Heavens forbid, madam! No, ſure, no reaſoning can be more juſt than yours. We ought certainly to deſpiſe malice if we cannot oppoſe it, and not make the incendiary's pen as fatal to our repoſe as the highwayman's piſtol.

Mrs. CROAKER.

O! then you think I'm quite right?

HONEYWOOD.

Perfectly right.

CROAKER.

A plague of plagues, we can't be both right. I ought to be ſorry, or I ought to be glad. My hat muſt be on my head, or my hat muſt be off.

Mrs. CROAKER.

Certainly, in two oppoſite opinions, if one be perfectly reaſonable, the other can't be perfectly right.

HONEYWOOD.

And why may not both be right, madam? Mr. Croaker in earneſtly ſeeking redreſs, and you in waiting the event with good humour? Pray let me ſee the letter again. I have it. This letter requires twenty guineas to be left at the bar of the Talbot inn. If it be indeed an incendiary letter, what if you and I, Sir, go there; and, when the writer comes to be paid his expected booty, ſeize him?

CROAKER.

My dear friend, it's the very thing; the very thing. While I walk by the door, you ſhall plant yourſelf in ambuſh near the bar; burſt out upon the miſcreant like a maſqued battery; extort a confeſſion at once, and ſo hang him up by ſurpriſe.

HONEYWOOD.

Yes; but I would not chuſe to exerciſe too much ſeverity. It is my maxim, Sir, that crimes generally puniſh themſelves.

CROAKER.

Well, but we may upbraid him a little, I ſuppoſe? [*Ironically.*

HONEYWOOD.

Aye, but not puniſh him too rigidly.

CROAKER.

Well, well, leave that to my own benevolence.

HONEYWOOD.

Well, I do: but remember that univerſal benevolence is the firſt law of nature.

[*Exeunt* Honeywood *and Mrs.* Croaker.

CROAKER.

Yes; and my univerſal benevolence will hang the dog, if he had as many necks as a hydra.

ACT

ACT THE FIFTH.

SCENE, an Inn.

Enter OLIVIA, JARVIS.

OLIVIA.

WELL, we have got ſafe to the Inn, however. Now, if the poſt-chaiſe were ready—

JARVIS.

The horſes are juſt finiſhing their oats; and, as they are not going to be married, they chooſe to take their own time.

OLIVIA.

You are for ever giving wrong motives to my impatience.

JARVIS.

Be as impatient as you will, the horſes muſt take their own time; beſides, you don't conſider, we have got no anſwer from our fellow-traveller yet. If we hear nothing from Mr. Leontine, we have only one way left us.

OLIVIA.

What way?

JARVIS.

The way home again.

OLIVIA.

Not ſo. I have made a reſolution to go, and nothing ſhall induce me to break it.

JARVIS.

Aye; reſolutions are well kept, when they jump with inclination. However, I'll go haſten things without. And I'll call, too, at the bar, to ſee if any thing ſhould be left for us there. Don't be in ſuch a plaguy hurry, madam, and we ſhall go the faſter, I promiſe you. [*Exit* Jarvis.

Enter LANDLADY.

LANDLADY.

What! Solomon, why don't you move? Pipes and tobacco for the Lamb there.—Will nobody anſwer? To the Dolphin; quick. The Angel has been outrageous this half hour. Did your ladyſhip call, madam?

OLIVIA.

No, madam.

LANDLADY.

I find, as you're for Scotland, madam—But that's no buſineſs of mine; married, or not married, I aſk no queſtions. To be ſure, we had a ſweet little couple ſet off from this two days ago for the ſame place. The gentleman, for a taylor, was, to be ſure, as fine a ſpoken taylor, as ever blew froth from a full

pot.

pot. And the young lady ſo baſhful, it was near half an hour before we could get her to finiſh a pint of raſberry between us.

OLIVIA.

But this gentleman and I are not going to be married, I aſſure you.

LANDLADY.

May be not. That's no buſineſs of mine; for certain, Scotch marriages ſeldom turn out. There was, of my own knowledge, Miſs Macfag, that married her father's footman.—Alack-a-day, ſhe and her huſband ſoon parted, and now keep ſeparate cellars in Hedge-lane.

OLIVIA.

A very pretty picture of what lies before me!

[*Aſide.*

Enter LEONTINE.

LEONTINE.

My dear Olivia, my anxiety, till you were out of danger, was too great to be reſiſted. I could not help coming to ſee you ſet out, though it expoſes us to a diſcovery.

OLIVIA.

May every thing you do prove as fortunate. Indeed, Leontine, we have been moſt cruelly diſappointed. Mr. Honeywood's bill upon the city has, it ſeems, been proteſted, and we have been utterly at a loſs how to proceed.

LEONTINE.

How! an offer of his own too. Sure, he could not mean to deceive us.

OLIVIA.

Depend upon his ſincerity; he only miſtook the deſire for the power of ſerving us. But let us think no more of it. I believe the poſt-chaiſe is ready by this.

LANDLADY.

Not quite yet: and, begging your ladyſhip's pardon, I don't think your ladyſhip quite ready for the poſt-chaiſe. The north road is a cold place, madam. I have a drop in the houſe of as pretty raſberry as ever was tipt over tongue. Juſt a thimble full to keep the wind off your ſtomach. To be ſure, the laſt couple we had here, they ſaid it was a perfect noſegay. Ecod, I ſent them both away as good natured—Up went the blinds, round went the wheels, and drive away poſt-boy, was the word.

Enter CROAKER.

CROAKER.

Well, while my friend Honeywood is upon the poſt of danger at the bar, it muſt be my buſineſs to have an eye about me here. I think I know an incendiary's look; for, wherever the devil makes a purchaſe, he never fails to ſet his mark. Ha! who have we here? My ſon and daughter! What can they be doing here!

LANDLADY.

I tell you, madam, it will do you good; I think I know by this time what's good for the north road. It's a raw night, madam.—Sir—

LEONTINE.

Not a drop more, good madam. I ſhould now take it as a greater favour, if you haſten the horſes, for I am afraid to be ſeen myſelf.

LANDLADY.

That ſhall be done. Wha, Solomon! are you all dead there? Wha, Solomon, I ſay! [*Exit, bawling.*

OLIVIA.

Well! I dread, leſt an expedition begun in fear, ſhould end in repentance.—Every moment we ſtay increaſes our danger, and adds to my apprehenſions.

LEONTINE.

There's no danger, truſt me, my dear; there can be none: if Honeywood has acted with honour, and kept my father, as he promiſed, in employment till we are out of danger, nothing can interrupt our journey.

OLIVIA.

I have no doubt of Mr. Honeywood's ſincerity, and even his deſires to ſerve us. My fears are from your father's ſuſpicions. A mind ſo diſpoſed to be alarmed without a cauſe, will be but too ready when there's a reaſon.

LEONTINE.

Why, let him, when we are out of his power. But believe me, Olivia, you have no great reaſon to dread his reſentment. His repining temper, as it does no manner of injury to himſelf, ſo will it never do harm to others. He only frets to keep himſelf employed, and ſcolds for his private amuſement.

OLIVIA.

I don't know that; but, I'm ſure, on ſome occaſions, it makes him look moſt ſhockingly.

CROAKER, diſcovering himſelf.

How does he look now?—How does he look now?

OLIVIA.

Ah!

LEONTINE.

Undone.

CROAKER.

How do I look now? Sir, I am your very humble ſervant. Madam, I am yours. What, you are going off, are you? Then, firſt, if you pleaſe, take a word or two from me with you before you go. Tell me firſt where you are going? and when you have told me that, perhaps, I ſhall know as little as I did before.

LEONTINE.

If that be ſo, our anſwer might but increaſe your diſpleaſure, without adding to your information.

CROAKER.

I want no information from you, puppy: and you too, good madam, what anſwer have you got? Eh!

(*A cry*

(*A cry without, stop him.*) I think I heard a noise. My friend Honeywood without—has he seized the incendiary? Ah, no, for now I hear no more on't.

LEONTINE.

Honeywood without! Then, Sir, it was Mr. Honeywood that directed you hither.

CROAKER.

No, Sir, it was Mr. Honeywood conducted me hither.

LEONTINE.

Is it possible?

CROAKER.

Possible! Why, he's in the house now, Sir: more anxious about me, than my own son, Sir.

LEONTINE.

Then, Sir, he's a villain.

CROAKER.

How, sirrah! a villain, because he takes most care of your father? I'll not bear it. I tell you I'll not bear it. Honeywood is a friend to the family, and I'll have him treated as such.

LEONTINE.

I shall study to repay his friendship as it deserves.

CROAKER.

Ah, rogue, if you knew how earnestly he entered into my griefs, and pointed out the means to detect them, you would love him as I do. (*A cry without, stop him.*) Fire and fury! they have seized the incendiary

cendiary: they have the villain, the incendiary in view. Stop him! ſtop an incendiary! a murderer; ſtop him! [*Exit.*

OLIVIA.

Oh, my terrors! What can this new tumult mean?

LEONTINE.

Some new mark, I ſuppoſe, of Mr. Honeywood's ſincerity. But we ſhall have ſatisfaction: he ſhall give me inſtant ſatisfaction.

OLIVIA.

It muſt not be, my Leontine, if you value my eſteem or my happineſs. Whatever be our fate, let us not add guilt to our misfortunes—Conſider that our innocence will ſhortly be all we have left us. You muſt forgive him.

LEONTINE.

Forgive him! Has he not in every inſtance betrayed us? Forced me to borrow money from him, which appears a mere trick to delay us: promiſed to keep my father engaged till we were out of danger, and here brought him to the very ſcene of our eſcape?

OLIVIA.

Don't be precipitate. We may yet be miſtaken.

Enter

Enter POSTBOY, dragging in JARVIS: HONEYWOOD entering ſoon after.

POSTBOY.

Aye, maſter, we have him faſt enough. Here is the incendiary dog. I'm entitled to the reward; I'll take my oath I ſaw him aſk for the money at the bar, and then run for it.

HONEYWOOD.

Come, bring him along. Let us ſee him. Let him learn to bluſh for his crimes. (*Diſcovering his miſtake.*) Death! what's here! Jarvis, Leontine, Olivia! What can all this mean?

JARVIS.

Why, I'll tell you what it means: that I was an old fool, and that you are my maſter—that's all.

HONEYWOOD.

Confuſion!

LEONTINE.

Yes, Sir, I find you have kept your word with me. After ſuch baſeneſs, I wonder how you can venture to ſee the man you have injured?

HONEYWOOD.

My dear Leontine, by my life, my honour—

LEONTINE.

Peace, peace, for ſhame; and do not continue to aggravate baſeneſs by hypocriſy. I know you, Sir, I know you,

Ho-

HONEYWOOD.

Why, won't you hear me! By all that's juſt, I knew not—

LEONTINE.

Hear you, Sir! to what purpoſe? I now ſee through all your low arts; your ever complying with every opinion; your never refuſing any requeſt; your friendſhip as common as a proſtitute's favours, and as fallacious; all theſe, Sir, have long been contemptible to the world, and are now perfectly ſo to me.

HONEYWOOD.

Ha! contemptible to the world! That reaches me. [*Aſide.*

LEONTINE.

All the ſeeming ſincerity of your profeſſions, I now find, were only allurements to betray; and all your ſeeming regret for their conſequences, only calculated to cover the cowardice of your heart. Draw, villain!

Enter CROAKER, out of breath.

CROAKER.

Where is the villain? Where is the incendiary? (*Seizing the poſtboy.*) Hold him faſt, the dog; he has the gallows in his face. Come, you dog, confeſs; confeſs all, and hang yourſelf.

POSTBOY.

Zounds! maſter, what do you throttle me for?

CROAKER,

CROAKER, beating him.

Dog, do you reſiſt; do you reſiſt?

POSTBOY.

Zounds! maſter, I'm not he; there's the man that we thought was the rogue, and turns out to be one of the company.

CROAKER.

How!

HONEYWOOD.

Mr. Croaker, we have all been under a ſtrange miſtake here; I find there is nobody guilty; it was all an error; entirely an error of our own.

CROAKER.

And I ſay, Sir, that you're in an error; for there's guilt and double guilt, a plot, a damned jeſüitical peſtilential plot, and I muſt have proof of it.

HONEYWOOD.

Do but hear me.

CROAKER.

What, you intend to bring 'em off, I ſuppoſe; I'll hear nothing.

HONEYWOOD.

Madam, you ſeem at leaſt calm enough to hear reaſon.

OLIVIA.

Excuſe me.

HONEYWOOD.

Good Jarvis, let me then explain it to you.

JARVIS.

JARVIS.

What ſignifies explanations, when the thing is done?

HONEYWOOD.

Will nobody hear me? Was there ever ſuch a ſet, ſo blinded by paſſion and prejudice! (*To the poſtboy.*) My good friend, I believe you'll be ſurpriſed, when I aſſure you—

POSTBOY.

Sure me nothing—I'm ſure of nothing but a good beating.

CROAKER.

Come, then, you, madam, if you ever hope for any favour or forgiveneſs, tell me ſincerely all you know of this affair.

OLIVIA.

Unhappily, Sir, I'm but too much the cauſe of your ſuſpicions: you ſee before you, Sir, one that with falſe pretences has ſtept into your family to betray it: not your daughter—

CROAKER.

Not my daughter!

OLIVIA.

Not your daughter—but a mean deceiver—who—ſupport me, I cannot—

HONEYWOOD.

Help, ſhe's going, give her air.

CROAKER.

CROAKER.

Aye, aye, take the young woman to the air; I would not hurt a hair of her head, whose ever daughter she may be—not so bad as that neither.

[*Exeunt all but* Croaker.

CROAKER.

Yes, yes, all's out; I now see the whole affair: my son is either married, or going to be so, to this lady, whom he imposed upon me as his sister. Aye, certainly so; and yet I don't find it afflicts me so much as one might think. There's the advantage of fretting away our misfortunes beforehand, we never feel them when they come.

Enter Miss RICHLAND and Sir WILLIAM.

Sir WILLIAM.

But how do you know, madam, that my nephew intends setting off from this place?

Miss RICHLAND.

My maid assured me he was come to this inn, and my own knowledge of his intending to leave the kingdom, suggested the rest. But what do I see, my guardian here before us! Who, my dear, Sir, could have expected meeting you here? to what accident do we owe this pleasure?

CROAKER.

To a fool, I believe.

Miss RICHLAND.

But, to what purpose did you come?

CROAKER.

To play the fool.

Miſs RICHLAND.

But, with whom?

CROAKER.

With greater fools than myſelf.

Miſs RICHLAND.

Explain.

CROAKER.

Why, Mr. Honeywood brought me here, to do nothing, now I am here; and my ſon is going to be married to I don't know who, that is here: ſo now you are as wiſe as I am.

Miſs RICHLAND.

Married! to whom, Sir?

CROAKER.

To Olivia; my daughter as I took her to be; but who the devil ſhe is, or whoſe daughter ſhe is, I know no more than the man in the moon.

Sir WILLIAM.

Then, Sir, I can inform you; and, though a ſtranger, yet you ſhall find me a friend to your family: it will be enough, at preſent, to aſſure you, that, both in point of birth and fortune, the young lady is at leaſt your ſon's equal. Being left by her father, Sir James Woodville——

CROAKER.

Sir James Woodville! What, of the weſt?

Sir

Sir William.

Being left by him, I ſay, to the care of a mercenary wretch, whoſe only aim was to ſecure her fortune to himſelf, ſhe was ſent to France, under pretence of education; and there every art was tried to fix her for life in a convent, contrary to her inclinations. Of this I was informed, upon my arrival at Paris; and, as I had been once her father's friend, I did all in my power to fruſtrate her guardian's baſe intentions. I had even meditated to reſcue her from his authority, when your ſon ſtept in with more pleaſing violence, gave her liberty, and you a daughter.

Croaker.

But I intend to have a daughter of my own chuſing, Sir. A young lady, Sir, whoſe fortune, by my intereſt with thoſe who have intereſt, will be double what my ſon has a right to expect. Do you know Mr. Lofty, Sir.

Sir William.

Yes, Sir; and know that you are deceived in him. But ſtep this way, and I'll convince you.

[Croaker *and* Sir William *ſeem to confer.*

Enter Honeywood.

Honeywood.

Obſtinate man, ſtill to perſiſt in his outrage! inſulted by him, deſpiſed by all, I now begin to grow contemptible, even to myſelf. How have I ſunk by too great an assiduity to please! How have I overtaxed all my abilities, lest the approbation of a single fool should escape me! But all is now over; I have survived my reputation, my fortune, my friendships, and nothing remains henceforward for me but solitude and repentance.

Miss RICHLAND.

Is it true, Mr. Honeywood, that you are setting off, without taking leave of your friends? The report is, that you are quitting England. Can it be?

HONEYWOOD.

Yes, madam; and though I am so unhappy as to have fallen under your displeasure, yet, thank Heaven, I leave you to happiness; to one who loves you, and deserves your love; to one who has power to procure you affluence, and generosity to improve your enjoyment of it.

Miss RICHLAND.

And are you sure, Sir, that the gentleman you mean is what you describe him?

HONEYWOOD.

I have the best assurances of it, his serving me. He does indeed deserve the highest happiness, and that is in your power to confer. As for me, weak and wavering as I have been, obliged by all, and incapable of serving any, what happiness can I find but in solitude? What hope but in being forgotten?

Miss

Miſs RICHLAND.

A thouſand! to live among friends that eſteem you, whoſe happineſs it will be to be permitted to oblige you.

HONEYWOOD.

No, madam; my reſolution is fixed. Inferiority among ſtrangers is eaſy; but among thoſe that once were equals, inſupportable. Nay, to ſhew you how far my reſolution can go, I can now ſpeak with calmneſs of my former follies, my vanity, my diſſipation, my weakneſs. I will even confeſs, that, among the number of my other preſumptions, I had the inſolence to think of loving you. Yes, madam, while I was pleading the paſſion of another, my heart was tortur'd with its own. But it is over, it was unworthy our friendſhip, and let it be forgotten.

Miſs RICHLAND.

You amaze me!

HONEYWOOD.

But you'll forgive it, I know you will; ſince the confeſſion ſhould not have come from me even now, but to convince you of the ſincerity of my intention of—never mentioning it more. [*Going.*

Miſs RICHLAND.

Stay, Sir, one moment—Ha! he here—

Enter Lofty.

Lofty.

Is the coaſt clear? None but friends. I have followed you here with a trifling piece of intelligence: but it goes no farther, things are not yet ripe for a diſcovery. I have ſpirits working at a certain board; your affair at the treaſury will be done in leſs than—a thouſand years. Mum!

Miſs Richland.

Sooner, Sir, I ſhould hope.

Lofty.

Why, yes, I believe it may, if it falls into proper hands, that know where to puſh and where to parry; that know how the land lies—eh, Honeywood.

Miſs Richland.

It has fallen into yours.

Lofty.

Well, to keep you no longer in ſuſpenſe, your thing is done. It is done, I ſay—that's all. I have juſt had aſſurances from Lord Neverout, that the claim has been examined, and found admiſſible. *Quietus* is the word, madam.

Honeywood.

But how! his lordſhip has been at Newmarket theſe ten days.

Lofty.

Indeed! Then Sir Gilbert Gooſe muſt have been moſt damnably miſtaken. I had it of him.

Miſs

Miſs RICHLAND.

He! why Sir Gilbert and his family have been in the country this month.

LOFTY.

This month! It muſt certainly be ſo—Sir Gilbert's letter did come to me from Newmarket, ſo that he muſt have met his lordſhip there; and ſo it came about. I have his letter about me; I'll read it to you. (*Taking out a large bundle.*) That's from Paoli of Corſica, that from the marquis of Squilachi.—Have you a mind to ſee a letter from count Poniatowſki, now king of Poland—Honeſt Pon— (*Searching.*) O, Sir, what are you here too? I'll tell you what, honeſt friend, if you have not abſolutely delivered my letter to Sir William Honeywood, you may return it. The thing will do without him.

Sir WILLIAM.

Sir, I have delivered it; and muſt inform you, it was received with the moſt mortifying contempt.

CROAKER.

Contempt! Mr. Lofty, what can that mean?

LOFTY.

Let him go on, let him go on, I ſay. You'll find it come to ſomething preſently.

Sir WILLIAM.

Yes, Sir, I believe you'll be amazed, if, after waiting ſome time in the anti-chamber, after being ſurveyed with inſolent curioſity by the paſſing ſervants, I was at laſt aſſured, that Sir William Honeywood knew no ſuch perſon, and I muſt certainly have been impoſed upon.

LOFTY.

Good; let me die; very good. Ha! ha! ha!

CROAKER.

Now, for my life, I can't find out half the goodneſs of it.

LOFTY.

You can't. Ha! ha!

CROAKER.

No, for the ſoul of me! I think it was as confounded a bad anſwer, as ever was ſent from one private gentleman to another.

LOFTY.

And ſo you can't find out the force of the meſſage? Why, I was in the houſe at that very time. Ha! ha! It was I that ſent that very anſwer to my own letter. Ha! ha!

CROAKER.

Indeed! How! why!

LOFTY.

In one word, things between Sir William and me muſt be behind the curtain. A party has many eyes. He ſides with lord Buzzard, I ſide with Sir Gilbert Gooſe. So that unriddles the myſtery.

CROAKER.

And ſo it does, indeed; and all my ſuſpicions are over.

LOFTY.

Your ſuſpicions! What, then, you have been ſuſpecting, you have been ſuſpecting have you? Mr. Croaker, you and I were friends; we are friends no longer. Never talk to me. It's over; I ſay, it's over.

CROAKER.

As I hope for your favour, I did not mean to offend. It eſcaped me. Don't be diſcompoſed.

LOFTY.

Zounds! Sir, but I am diſcompoſed, and will be diſcompoſed. To be treated thus! Who am I! Was it for this, I have been dreaded both by ins and outs! Have I been libelled in the Gazetteer, and praiſed in the St. James's? have I been chaired at Wildman's, and a ſpeaker at Merchant-Taylors Hall? have I had my hand to addreſſes, and my head in the print-ſhops; and talk to me of ſuſpects?

CROAKER.

My dear Sir, be pacified. What can you have but aſking pardon?

LOFTY.

Sir, I will not be pacified—Suſpects! Who am I! To be uſed thus! Have I paid court to men in favour, to ſerve my friends; the lords of the treaſury, Sir William Honeywood, and the reſt of the gang, and talk to me of ſuſpects! Who am I, I ſay, who am I!

Sir William.

Since, Sir, you are ſo preſſing for an anſwer, I'll tell you who you are. A gentleman, as well acquainted with politics, as with men in power; as well acquainted with perſons of faſhion, as with modeſty; with lords of the treaſury, as with truth; and with all, as you are with Sir William Honeywood. I am Sir William Honeywood.

[*Diſcovering his enſigns of the Bath.*

Croaker.

Sir William Honeywood!

Honeywood.

Aſtoniſhment! my uncle! [*Aſide.*

Lofty.

So then, my confounded genius has been all this time only leading me up to the garret, in order to fling me out of the window.

Croaker.

What, Mr. Importance, and are theſe your works! Suſpect you? You who have been dreaded by the ins and outs: you, who have had your hand to addreſſes, and your head ſtuck up in printſhops. If you were ſerved right, you ſhould have your head ſtuck up in the pillory.

Lofty.

Aye, ſtick it where you will; for, by the Lord, it cuts but a very poor figure where it ſticks at preſent.

Sir

Sir WILLIAM.

Well, Mr. Croaker, I hope you now ſee how incapable this gentleman is of ſerving you, and how little Miſs Richland has to expect from his influence.

CROAKER.

Aye, Sir, too well I ſee it; and I can't but ſay I have had ſome boding of it theſe ten days. So, I'm reſolved, ſince my ſon has placed his affections on a lady of moderate fortune, to be ſatisfied with his choice, and not run the hazard of another Mr. Lofty, in helping him to a better.

Sir WILLIAM.

I approve your reſolution; and here they come, to receive a confirmation of your pardon and conſent.

Enter Mrs. CROAKER, JARVIS, LEONTINE, and OLIVIA.

Mrs. CROAKER.

Where's my huſband! Come, come, lovey, you muſt forgive them. Jarvis here has been to tell me the whole affair; and, I ſay, you muſt forgive them. Our own was a ſtolen match, you know, my dear; and we never had any reaſon to repent of it.

CROAKER.

CROAKER.

I wiſh we could both ſay ſo. However, this gentleman, Sir William Honeywood, has been beforehand with you, in obtaining their pardon. So, if the two poor fools have a mind to marry, I think we can tack them together without croſſing the Tweed for it. [*Joining their hands.*

LEONTINE.

How bleſt and unexpected! What, what can we ſay to ſuch goodneſs! But, our future obedience ſhall be the beſt reply. And, as for this gentleman, to whom we owe—

Sir WILLIAM.

Excuſe me, Sir, if I interrupt your thanks, as I have here an intereſt that calls me. *Turning to* Honeywood.) Yes, Sir, you are ſurpriſed to ſee me; and I own that a deſire of correcting your follies led me hither. I ſaw, with indignation, the errors of a mind that only ſought applauſe from others; that eaſineſs of diſpoſition, which, though inclined to the right, had not courage to condemn the wrong. I ſaw, with regret, thoſe ſplendid errors, that ſtill took name from ſome neighbouring duty. Your charity, that was but injuſtice; your benevolence, that was but weakneſs; and your friendſhip, but credulity. I ſaw, with regret, great talents, and extenſive learning, only employed to add ſprightlineſs to error, and encreaſe your perplexities. I ſaw your mind with a thouſand natural charms: but,

the

the greatneſs of its beauty ſerved only to heighten my pity for it's proſtitution.

HONEYWOOD.

Ceaſe to upbraid me, Sir: I have for ſome time but too ſtrongly felt the juſtice of your reproaches. But there is one way ſtill left me. Yes, Sir, I have determined this very hour, to quit for ever a place where I have made myſelf the voluntary ſlave of all; and to ſeek among ſtrangers that fortitude which may give ſtrength to the mind, and marſhal all its diſſipated virtues. Yet, ere I depart, permit me to ſolicit favour for this gentleman; who, notwithſtanding what has happened, has laid me under the moſt ſignal obligations. Mr. Lofty——

LOFTY.

Mr. Honeywood, I'm reſolved upon a reformation, as well as you. I now begin to find, that the man who firſt invented the art of ſpeaking truth was a much cunninger fellow than I thought him. And, to prove that I deſign to ſpeak truth for the future, I muſt now aſſure you, that you owe your late enlargement to another; as, upon my ſoul, I had no hand in the matter. So now if any of the company has a mind for preferment, he may take my place, I'm determined to reſign. [*Exit.*

HONEYWOOD.

How have I been deceived!

Sir

Sir William.

No, Sir, you have been obliged to a kinder, fairer friend for that favour. To Miſs Richland. Would ſhe complete our joy, and make the man ſhe has honoured by her friendſhip happy in her love, I ſhould then forget all, and be as bleſt as the welfare of my deareſt kinſman can make me.

Miſs Richland.

After what is paſt, it would be but affectation to pretend to indifference. Yes, I will own an attachment, which, I find, was more than friendſhip. And, if my intreaties cannot alter his reſolution to quit the country, I will even try if my hand has not power to detain him. [*Giving her hand.*

Honeywood.

Heavens! how can I have deſerved all this? How expreſs my happineſs, my gratitude! A moment, like this, overpays an age of apprehenſion.

Croaker.

Well, now I ſee content in every face; but Heaven ſend we be all better this day three months!

Sir William.

Henceforth, nephew, learn to reſpect yourſelf. He who ſeeks only for applauſe from without, has all his happineſs in another's keeping.

Ho-

HONEYWOOD.

Yes, Sir, I now too plainly perceive my errors. My vanity in attempting to pleaſe all, by fearing to offend any. My meanneſs in approving folly, leſt fools ſhould diſapprove. Henceforth, therefore, it ſhall be my ſtudy to reſerve my pity for real diſtreſs; my friendſhip for true merit; and my love for her, who firſt taught me what it is to be happy.

EPILOGUE.*

SPOKEN BY

MRS. BULKLEY.

As puffing quacks ſome caitiff wretch procure
To ſwear the pill, or drop, has wrought a cure;
Thus, on the ſtage, our play-wrights ſtill depend
For Epilogues and Prologues on ſome friend,
Who knows each art of coaxing up the town,
And make full many a bitter pill go down.
Conſcious of this, our bard has gone about,
And teaz'd each rhyming friend to help him out.
An Epilogue, things can't go on without it;
It could not fail, would you but ſet about it.
Young man, cries one, (a bard laid up in clover)
Alas, young man, my writing days are over;
Let boys play tricks, and kick the ſtraw, not I;
Your brother doctor there, perhaps, may try.
What I! dear Sir, the doctor interpoſes;
What, plant my thiſtle, Sir, among his roſes!

* The author, in expectation of an Epilogue from a friend at Oxford, deferred writing one himſelf till the very laſt hour. What is here offered, owes all it's ſucceſs to the graceful manner of the actreſs who ſpoke it.

No,

No, no, I've other contests to maintain:
To-night I head our troops at Warwick-lane.
Go, ask your manager—Who, me! Your pardon;
Those things are not our forte at Covent-garden.
Our author's friends, thus plac'd at happy distance,
Give him good words indeed, but no assistance.
As some unhappy wight, at some new play,
At the pit door stands elbowing away,
While oft, with many a smile, and many a shrug,
He eyes the centre, where his friends sit snug;
His simpering friends, with pleasure in their eyes,
Sinks as he sinks, and as he rises rise:
He nods, they nod; he cringes, they grimace;
But not a soul will budge to give him place.
Since then, unhelp'd, our bard must now conform
"To 'bide the pelting of this pitt'less storm,"
Blame where you must, be candid where you can,
And be each critic the *Good-natur'd Man*.

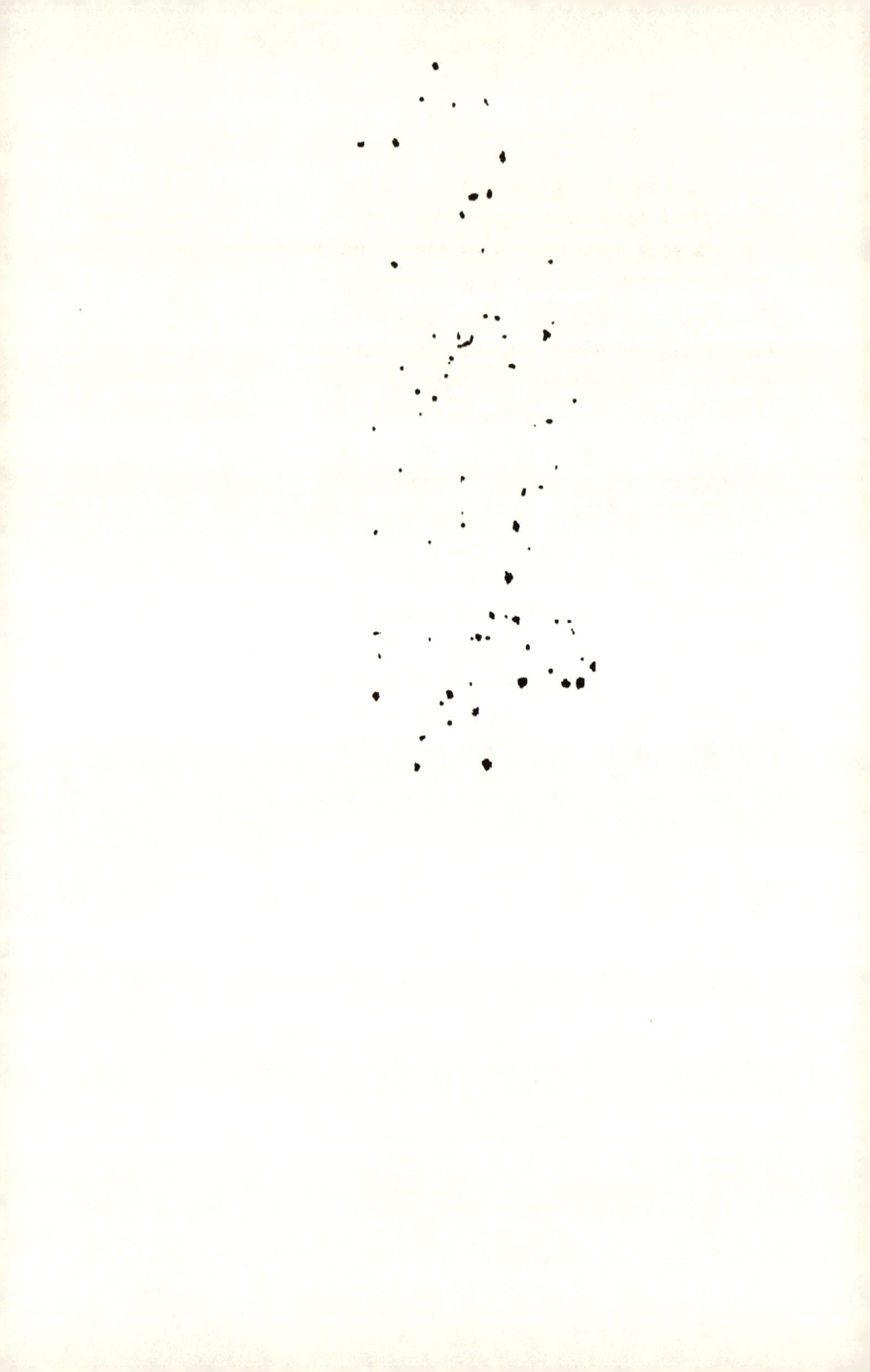

SHE STOOPS TO CONQUER:

O R,

THE MISTAKES OF A NIGHT.

A

C O M E D Y.

AS IT IS ACTED AT THE

THEATRE-ROYAL,

IN

COVENT-GARDEN.

FIRST PRINTED IN MDCCLXXIII.

TO

SAMUEL JOHNSON, L. L. D.

DEAR SIR,

BY inſcribing this ſlight performance to you, I do not mean ſo much to compliment you as myſelf. It may do me ſome honour to inform the public, that I have lived many years in intimacy with you. It may ſerve the intereſts of mankind alſo to inform them that the greateſt wit may be found in a character, without impairing the moſt unaffected piety.

I have, particularly, reaſon to thank you for your partiality to this performance. The undertaking a comedy, not merely ſentimental, was very dangerous; and Mr. Colman, who ſaw this piece in its various ſtages, always thought it ſo. However, I ventured to truſt it to the public; and, though it was neceſſarily delayed till late in the ſeaſon, I have every reaſon to be grateful. I am,

DEAR SIR,

YOUR MOST SINCERE

FRIEND AND ADMIRER,

OLIVER GOLDSMITH.

PROLOGUE.

BY

DAVID GARRICK, ESQ.

Enter Mr. Woodward, dreſſed in Black, and holding a handkerchief to his Eyes.

EXCUSE me, Sirs, I pray—I can't yet ſpeak—
I'm crying now—and have been all the week.
" 'Tis not alone this mourning ſuit," good maſters;
" I've that within"—for which there are no plaſters!
Pray, would you know the reaſon why I'm crying?
The comic muſe, long ſick, is now a dying!
And if ſhe goes, my tears will never ſtop;
For as a play'r, I can't ſqueeze out one drop:
I am undone, that's all—ſhall loſe my bread—
I'd rather, but that's nothing—loſe my head.
When the ſweet maid is laid upon the bier,
Shuter and I ſhall be chief mourners here.
To her a mawkiſh drab of ſpurious breed,
Who deals in Sentimentals, will ſucceed!
Poor Ned and I are dead to all intents;
We can as ſoon ſpeak Greek as Sentiments!
Both nervous grown, to keep our ſpirits up,
We now and then take down a hearty cup.

What

What ſhall we do?—If Comedy forſake us!
They'll turn us out, and no one elſe will take us.
But, why can't I be moral?—Let me try—
My heart thus preſſing—fix'd my face and eye—
With a ſententious look, that nothing means,
(Faces are blocks, in ſentimental ſcenes)
Thus I begin—"All is not gold that glitters,
"Pleaſures ſeem ſweet, but prove a glaſs of bitters.
"When ign'rance enters, folly is at hand:
"Learning is better far than houſe and land.
"Let not your virtue trip, who trips may ſtumble,
"And virtue is not virtue, if ſhe tumble."
I give it up—morals won't do for me;
To make you laugh, I muſt play tragedy.
One hope remains—hearing the maid was ill,
A Doctor comes this night to ſhew his ſkill.
To cheer her heart, and give your muſcles motion,
He, in Five Draughts prepar'd, preſents a potion:
A kind of magic charm—for be aſſur'd,
If you will ſwallow it, the maid is cur'd:
But deſp'rate the Doctor, and her caſe is,
If you reject the doſe, and make wry faces!
This truth he boaſts, will boaſt it while he lives,
No pois'nous drugs are mix'd in what he gives.
Should he ſucceed, you'll give him his degree:
If not, within he will receive no fee!
The college you, muſt his pretenſions back,
Pronounce him Regular, or dub him Quack.

DRAMATIS PERSONÆ.

MEN.

Sir Charles Marlow,	Mr. Gardner.
Young Marlow, (his ſon)	Mr. Lewes.
Hardcaſtle,	Mr. Shuter.
Haſtings,	Mr. Dubellamy.
Tony Lumpkin,	Mr. Quick.
Diggory,	Mr. Saunders.

WOMEN.

Mrs. Hardcaſtle,	Mrs. Green.
Miſs Hardcaſtle,	Mrs. Bulkley.
Miſs Neville,	Mrs. Kniveton.
Maid,	Miſs Willems.

Landlord, Servants, &c. &c.

SHE STOOPS TO CONQUER:

OR,

THE MISTAKES OF A NIGHT.

ACT THE FIRST.

SCENE, a Chamber in an old-fashioned House.

Enter Mrs. HARDCASTLE and Mr. HARDCASTLE.

Mrs. HARDCASTLE.

I VOW, Mr. Hardcastle, you're very particular. Is there a creature in the whole country, but ourselves, that does not take a trip to town now and then, to rub off the rust a little? There's the two Miss Hoggs, and our neighbour, Mrs. Grigsby, go to take a month's polishing every winter.

HARDCASTLE.

Aye, and bring back vanity and affectation to last them the whole year. I wonder why London cannot keep its own fools at home! In my time, the follies of the town crept ſlowly among us, but now they travel faſter than a ſtage-coach. Its fopperies come down, not only as inſide paſſengers, but in the very baſket.

Mrs. HARDCASTLE.

Aye, your times were fine times, indeed; you have been telling us of them for many a long year. Here we live in an old rumbling manſion, that looks for all the world like an inn, but that we never ſee company. Our beſt viſitors are old Mrs. Oddfiſh, the curate's wife, and little Cripplegate, the lame dancing-maſter: and all our entertainment your old ſtories of prince Eugène and the duke of Marlborough. I hate ſuch old-faſhioned trumpery.

HARDCASTLE.

And I love it. I love every thing that's old: old friends, old times, old manners, old books, old wine; and, I believe, Dorothy, (*taking her hand*) you'll own I have been pretty fond of an old wife.

Mrs. HARDCASTLE.

Lord, Mr. Hardcaſtle, you're for ever at your Dorothy's and your old wife's. You may be a Darby, but I'll be no Joan, I promiſe you. I'm not ſo old as you'd make me, by more than one good year. Add twenty to twenty, and make money of that.

HARDCASTLE.

Let me ſee; twenty added to twenty, makes juſt fifty and ſeven.

Mrs.

Mrs. HARDCASTLE.

It's falſe, Mr. Hardcaſtle: I was but twenty when I was brought to bed of Tony, that I had by Mr. Lumpkin, my firſt huſband; and he's not come to years of diſcretion yet.

HARDCASTLE.

Nor ever will, I dare anſwer for him. Aye, you have taught him finely.

Mrs. HARDCASTLE.

No matter, Tony Lumpkin has a good fortune. My ſon is not to live by his learning. I don't think a boy wants much learning to ſpend fifteen hundred a year.

HARDCASTLE.

Learning, quotha! A mere compoſition of tricks and miſchief.

Mrs. HARDCASTLE.

Humour, my dear: nothing but humour. Come, Mr. Hardcaſtle, you muſt allow the boy a little humour.

HARDCASTLE.

I'd ſooner allow him an horſe-pond. If burning the footmens ſhoes, frighting the maids, and worrying the kittens, be humour, he has it. It was but yeſterday he faſtened my wig to the back of my chair, and when I went to make a bow, I popt my bald head in Mrs. Frizzle's face.

Mrs. HARDCASTLE.

And am I to blame? The poor boy was always too ſickly to do any good. A ſchool would be his death.

death. When he comes to be a little ſtronger, who knows what a year or two's Latin may do for him?

HARDCASTLE.

Latin for him! A cat and fiddle. No, no, the alehouſe and the ſtable are the only ſchools he'll ever go to.

Mrs. HARDCASTLE.

Well, we muſt not ſnub the poor boy now, for I believe we ſhan't have him long among us. Any body that looks in his face may ſee he's conſumptive.

HARDCASTLE.

Aye, if growing too fat be one of the ſymptoms.

Mrs. HARDCASTLE.

He coughs ſometimes.

HARDCASTLE.

Yes, when his liquor goes the wrong way.

Mrs. HARDCASTLE.

I'm actually afraid of his lungs.

HARDCASTLE.

And truly ſo am I; for he ſometimes whoops like a ſpeaking trumpet— (*Tony hallooing behind the ſcenes*)—O there he goes—A very conſumptive figure, truly.

Enter TONY, croſſing the Stage.

Mrs. HARDCASTLE.

Tony, where are you going, my charmer? Won't you give papa and I a little of your company, lovee?

TONY.

TONY.

I'm in haſte, mother, I cannot ſtay.

Mrs. HARDCASTLE.

You ſhan't venture out this raw evening, my dear: You look moſt ſhockingly.

TONY.

I can't ſtay, I tell you. The three pigeons expects me down every moment. There's ſome fun going forward.

HARDCASTLE.

Aye; the ale-houſe, the old place: I thought ſo.

Mrs. HARDCASTLE.

A low, paltry ſet of fellows.

TONY.

Not ſo low neither. There's Dick Muggins the exciſeman, Jack Slang the horſe doctor, little Aminadab that grinds the muſic box, and Tom Twiſt that ſpins the pewter platter.

Mrs. HARDCASTLE.

Pray, my dear, diſappoint them for one night at leaſt.

TONY.

As for diſappointing them I ſhould not ſo much mind; but I can't abide to diſappoint myſelf.

Mrs. HARDCASTLE.

(*Detaining him*) You ſhan't go.

TONY.

I will, I tell you.

Mrs. HARDCASTLE.

I ſay you ſhan't.

TONY.

We'll ſee which is ſtrongeſt, you or I.

[*Exit, hauling her out.*

HARDCASTLE, ſolus.

Aye, there goes a pair that only ſpoil each other. But is not the whole age in a combination to drive ſenſe and diſcretion out of doors? There's my pretty darling Kate; the faſhions of the times have almoſt infected her too. By living a year or two in town, ſhe is as fond of gauze, and French frippery, as the beſt of them.

Enter Miſs HARDCASTLE.

HARDCASTLE.

Bleſſings on my pretty innocence! dreſt out as uſual, my Kate. Goodneſs! What a quantity of ſuperfluous ſilk haſt thou got about thee, girl! I could never teach the fools of this age, that the indigent world could be cloathed out of the trimmings of the vain.

Miſs HARDCASTLE.

You know our agreement, Sir. You allow me the morning to receive and pay viſits, and to dreſs in my own manner; and in the evening, I put on my houſewife's dreſs to pleaſe you.

HARD-

HARDCASTLE.

Well, remember I inſiſt on the terms of our agrement; and, by the bye, I believe I ſhall have occaſion to try your obedience this very evening.

Miſs HARDCASTLE.

I proteſt, Sir, I don't comprehend your meaning.

HARDCASTLE.

Then, to be plain with you, Kate, I expect the young gentleman I have choſen to be your huſband from town this very day. I have his father's letter, in which he informs me his ſon is ſet out, and that he intends to follow himſelf ſhortly after.

Miſs HARDCASTLE.

Indeed! I wiſh I had known ſomething of this before. Bleſs me, how ſhall I behave? It's a thouſand to one I ſhan't like him; our meeting will be ſo formal, and ſo like a thing of buſineſs, that I ſhall find no room for friendſhip or eſteem.

HARDCASTLE.

Depend upon it, child, I'll never controul your choice; but Mr. Marlow, whom I have pitched upon, is the ſon of my old friend, Sir Charles Marlow, of whom you have heard me talk ſo often. The young gentleman has been bred a ſcholar, and is deſigned for an employment in the ſervice of his country. I am told he's a man of an excellent underſtanding,

Miſs

Miss HARDCASTLE.

Is he?

HARDCASTLE.

Very generous.

Miss HARDCASTLE.

I believe I shall like him.

HARDCASTLE.

Young and brave.

Miss HARDCASTLE.

I'm sure I shall like him.

HARDCASTLE.

And very handsome.

Miss HARDCASTLE.

My dear papa, say no more, (*kissing his hand*) he's mine, I'll have him.

HARDCASTLE.

And, to crown all, Kate, he's one of the most bashful and reserved young fellows in all the world.

Miss HARDCASTLE.

Eh! you have frozen me to death again. That word reserved, has undone all the rest of his accomplishments. A reserved lover, it is said, always makes a suspicious husband,

HARDCASTLE.

On the contrary, modesty seldom resides in a breast that is not enriched with nobler virtues. It was the very feature in his character that first struck me.

Miss

Miſs HARDCASTLE.

He muſt have more ſtriking features to catch me, I promiſe you. However, if he be ſo young, ſo handſome, and ſo every thing, as you mention, I believe he'll do ſtill. I think I'll have him.

HARDCASTLE.

Aye, Kate, but there is ſtill an obſtacle. It's more than an even wager, he may not have you.

Miſs HARDCASTLE.

My dear papa, why will you mortify one ſo?—Well, if he refuſes, inſtead of breaking my heart at his indifference, I'll only break my glaſs for its flattery. Set my cap to ſome newer faſhion, and look out for ſome leſs difficult admirer.

HARDCASTLE.

Bravely reſolved! In the mean time I'll go prepare the ſervants for his reception; as we ſeldom ſee company, they want as much training as a company of recruits, the firſt day's muſter. [*Exit.*

Miſs HARDCASTLE, ſola.

Lud, this news of papa's puts me all in a flutter. Young, handſome; theſe he put laſt? but I put them foremoſt. Senſible, good-natured; I like all that. But then reſerved, and ſheepiſh, that's much againſt him. Yet can't he be cured of his timidity, by being taught to be proud of his wife? Yes, and can't I—But I vow I'm diſpoſing of the huſband, before I have ſecur'd the lover.

Enter

Enter Miſs NEVILLE.

Miſs HARDCASTLE.

I'm glad you're come, Neville, my dear. Tell me, Conſtance, how do I look this evening? Is there any thing whimſical about me? Is it one of my well looking days, child? am I in face today?

Miſs NEVILLE.

Perfectly, my dear. Yet now I look again—bleſs me!—ſure no accident has happened among the canary birds or the gold fiſhes. Has your brother or the cat been medling? or has the laſt novel been too moving?

Miſs HARDCASTLE.

No; nothing of all this. I have been threatened —I can ſcarce get it out—I have been threatened with a lover.

Miſs NEVILLE.

And his name——

Miſs HARDCASTLE.

Is Marlow.

Miſs NEVILLE.

Indeed!

Miſs HARDCASTLE.

The ſon of Sir Charles Marlow.

Miſs NEVILLE.

As I live, the moſt intimate friend of Mr. Haſtings, my admirer. They are never aſunder. I

believe

believe you muſt have ſeen him when we lived in town.

Miſs HARDCASTLE.

Never.

Miſs NEVILLE.

He's a very ſingular character, I aſſure you. Among women of reputation and virtue, he is the modeſteſt man alive; but his acquaintance give him a very different character among creatures of another ſtamp: you underſtand me.

Miſs HARDCASTLE.

An odd character, indeed. I ſhall never be able to manage him. What ſhall I do? Pſhaw, think no more of him, but truſt to occurrences for ſucceſs. But how goes on your own affair, my dear? has my mother been courting you for my brother Tony, as uſual?

Miſs NEVILLE.

I have juſt come from one of our agreeable tête-a-têtes. She has been ſaying a hundred tender things, and ſetting off her pretty monſter as the very pink of perfection.

Miſs HARDCASTLE.

And her partiality is ſuch, that ſhe actually thinks him ſo. A fortune like yours is no ſmall temptation. Beſides, as ſhe has the ſole management of it, I'm not ſurprized to ſee her unwilling to let it go out of the family.

Miſs Neville.

A fortune like mine, which chiefly conſiſts in jewels, is no ſuch mighty temptation. But at any rate if my dear Haſtings be but conſtant, I make no doubt to be too hard for her at laſt. However, I let her ſuppoſe that I am in love with her ſon, and ſhe never once dreams that my affections are fixed upon another.

Miſs Hardcastle.

My good brother holds out ſtoutly. I could almoſt love him for hating you ſo.

Miſs Neville.

It is a good-natured creature at bottom, and I'm ſure would wiſh to ſee me married to any body but himſelf. But my aunt's bell rings for our afternoon's walk round the improvements. Allons! Courage is neceſſary as our affairs are critical.

Miſs Hardcastle.

"Would it were bed time and all were well."

[*Exeunt.*

Scene, an Ale-houſe Room. Several ſhabby fellows, with punch and tobacco. Tony at the Head of the Table, a little higher than the reſt; a mallet in his hand.

Omnes.

Hurrea! hurrea! hurrea! bravo!

First Fellow,

Now gentlemen, ſilence for a ſong. The 'ſquire is going to knock himſelf down for a ſong.

Omnes.

OMNES.

Aye, a ſong, a ſong!

TONY.

Then I'll ſing you, gentlemen, a ſong I made upon this ale-houſe, the Three Pigeons.

SONG.

Let ſchool-maſters puzzle their brain,
  With grammar, and nonſenſe, and learning;
Good liquor, I ſtoutly maintain,
  Gives *genus* a better diſcerning.
Let them brag of their heatheniſh gods,
  Their Lethes, their Styxes, and Stygians;
Their qui's, and their quæ's, and their quod's,
  They're all but a parcel of pigeons.
      Toroddle, toroddle, toroll.

When methodiſt preachers come down,
  A preaching that drinking is ſinful,
I'll wager the raſcals a crown,
  They always preach beſt with a ſkinful.
But when you come down with your pence,
  For a ſlice of their ſcurvy religion,
I'll leave it to all men of ſenſe,
  But you my good friend are the pigeon.
      Toroddle, toroddle, toroll.

Then come put the jorum about,
  And let us be merry and clever,
Our hearts and our liquors are ſtout,
  Here's the three jolly pigeons for ever.

Let ſome cry up woodcock or hare,
Your buſtards, your ducks, and your widgeons;
But of all the birds in the air,
Here's a health to the three jolly pigeons.
Toroddle, toroddle, toroll.

OMNES.

Bravo, bravo!

FIRST FELLOW.

The 'ſquire has got ſpunk in him.

SECOND FFLLOW.

I loves to hear him ſing, bekeays he never gives us nothing that's low.

THIRD FELLOW.

O damn any thing that's low, I cannot bear it.

FOURTH FELLOW.

The genteel thing is the genteel thing at any time. If ſo be that a gentleman bees in a concatenation accordingly.

THIRD FELLOW.

I like the maxum of it, maſter Muggins. What, though I am obligated to dance a bear, a man may be a gentleman for all that. May this be my poiſon if my bear ever dances but to the very genteeleſt of tunes. "Water Parted," or "the minuet in Ariadne."

SECOND FELLOW.

What a pity it is the 'ſquire is not come to his own. It would be well for all the publicans within ten miles round of him.

TONY.

TONY.

Ecod and ſo it would, maſter Slang. I'd then ſhew what it was to keep choice of company.

SECOND FELLOW.

O he takes after his own father for that. To be ſure old 'ſquire Lumpkin was the fineſt gentleman I ever ſet my eyes on. For winding the ſtraight horn, or beating a thicket for a hare, or a wench, he never had his fellow. It was a ſaying in the place, that he kept the beſt horſes, dogs, and girls in the whole county.

TONY.

Ecod, and when I'm of age, I'll be no baſtard, I promiſe you. I have been thinking of Bett Bouncer and the miller's grey mare to begin with. But, come, my boys, drink about and be merry, for you pay no reckoning. Well, Stingo, what's the matter?

Enter LANDLORD.

LANDLORD.

There be two gentlemen in a poſt-chaiſe at the door. They have loſt their way upo' the foreſt; and they are talking ſomething about Mr. Hardcaſtle.

TONY.

As ſure as can be, one of them muſt be the gentleman that's coming down to court my ſiſter. Do they ſeem to be Londoners?

LANDLORD.

I believe they may. They look woundily like Frenchmen.

TONY.

Then deſire them to ſtep this way, and I'll ſet them right in a twinkling. (*Exit Landlord.*) Gentlemen, as they may'nt be good enough company for you, ſtep down for a moment, and I'll be with you in the ſqueezing of a lemon. [*Exeunt mob.*

TONY, ſolus.

Father-in-law has been calling me whelp, and hound, this half year. Now, if I pleaſed, I could be ſo revenged upon the old grumbletonian. But then I'm afraid—afraid of what! I ſhall ſoon be worth fifteen hundred a year, and let him frighten me out of that if he can.

Enter LANDLORD, conducting MARLOW and HASTINGS.

MARLOW.

What a tedious uncomfortable day have we had of it! We were told it was but forty miles acroſs the country, and we have come above threeſcore.

HASTINGS.

And all, Marlow, from that unaccountable reſerve of yours, that would not let us inquire more frequently on the way.

MAR-

MARLOW.

I own, Haſtings, I am unwilling to lay myſelf under an obligation to every one I meet; and often ſtand the chance of an unmannerly anſwer.

HASTINGS.

At preſent, however, we are not likely to receive any anſwer.

TONY.

No offence, gentlemen. But I'm told you have been inquiring for one Mr. Hardcaſtle in thoſe parts. Do you know what part of the country you are in?

HASTINGS.

Not in the leaſt, Sir, but ſhould thank you for information.

TONY.

Nor the way you came?

HASTINGS.

No, Sir? but if you can inform us——

TONY.

Why, gentlemen, if you know neither the road you are going, nor where you are, nor the road you came, the firſt thing I have to inform you is, that—you have loſt your way.

MARLOW.

We wanted no ghoſt to tell us that.

TONY.

Pray, gentlemen, may I be ſo bold as to aſk the place from whence you came?

MARLOW.

That's not neceſſary towards directing us where we are to go.

TONY.

No offence; but queſtion for queſtion is all fair, you know. Pray, gentlemen, is not this ſame Hardcaſtle a croſs-grain'd, oldfaſhion'd, whimſical fellow, with an ugly face; a daughter, and a pretty ſon?

HASTINGS.

We have not ſeen the gentleman, but he has the family you mention.

TONY.

The daughter, a tall, trapeſing, trolloping, talkative maypole—the ſon, a pretty, well-bred, agreeable youth, that every body is fond of.

MARLOW.

Our information differs in this. The daughter is ſaid to be well-bred and beautiful; the ſon, an aukward booby, reared up, and ſpoiled at his mother's apron-ſtring.

TONY.

He-he-hem!—Then, gentlemen, all I have to tell you is, that you won't reach Mr. Hardcaſtle's houſe this night, I believe.

HASTINGS.

Unfortunate!

TONY.

It's a damn'd long, dark, boggy, dirty, dangerous way. Stingo, tell the gentlemen the way to

Mr.

Mr. Hardcaſtle's! (*Winking upon the Landlord.*) Mr. Hardcaſtle's of Quagmire Marſh, you underſtand me.

LANDLORD.

Maſter Hardcaſtle's! Lock-a-daiſy, my maſters, you're come a deadly deal wrong! When you came to the bottom of the hill, you ſhould have croſs'd down Squaſh-lane.

MARLOW.

Croſs down Squaſh-lane!

LANDLORD.

Then you were to keep ſtraight forward, 'till you came to four roads.

MARLOW.

Come to where four roads meet!

TONY.

Aye; but you muſt be ſure to take only one of them.

MARLOW.

O Sir, you're facetious.

TONY.

Then keeping to the right, you are to go ſideways till you come upon Crack-ſkull common: there you muſt look ſharp for the track of the wheel, and go forward, 'till you come to farmer Murrain's barn. Coming to the farmer's barn, you are to turn to the right, and then to the left, and then to the right about again, till you find out the old mill.

MAR-

MARLOW.

Zounds, man! we could as ſoon find out the longitude!

HASTINGS.

What's to be done, Marlow?

MARLOW.

This houſe promiſes but a poor reception; though perhaps the landlord can accommodate us.

LANDLORD.

Alack, maſter, we have but one ſpare bed in the whole houſe.

TONY.

And to my knowledge, that's taken up by three lodgers already. (*After a pauſe, in which the reſt ſeem diſconcerted*) I have hit it. Don't you think, Stingo, our landlady could accommodate the gentlemen by the fire-ſide, with——three chairs and a bolſter?

HASTINGS.

I hate ſleeping by the fire-ſide.

MARLOW.

And I deteſt your three chairs and a bolſter.

TONY.

You do, do you!—then let me ſee—what—if you go on a mile further, to the Buck's Head; the old Buck's Head on the hill, one of the beſt inns in the whole county?

HASTINGS.

O ho! ſo we have eſcaped an adventure for this night, however.

LAND-

LANDLORD.

(*Apart to Tony*) Sure, you ben't ſending them to your father's as an inn, be you?

TONY.

Mum, you fool you. Let them find that out. (*To them.*) You have only to keep on ſtraight forward, till you come to a large old houſe by the road ſide. You'll ſee a pair of large horns over the door. That's the ſign. Drive up the yard, and call ſtoutly about you.

HASTINGS.

Sir, we are obliged to you. The ſervants can't miſs the way?

TONY.

No, no: but I tell you though, the landlord is rich, and going to leave off buſineſs; ſo he wants to be thought a gentleman, ſaving your preſence, he! he! he! He'll be for giving you his company, and ecod if you mind him, he'll perſuade you that his mother was an alderman, and his aunt a juſtice of peace.

LANDLORD.

A troubleſome old blade to be ſure; but a keeps as good wines and beds as any in the whole country.

MARLOW.

Well, if he ſupplies us with theſe, we ſhall want no further connection. We are to turn to the right, did you ſay?

TONY.

TONY.

No, no; ſtraight forward. I'll juſt ſtep myſelf, and ſhew you a piece of the way. (*To the landlord*) Mum.

LANDLORD.

Ah, bleſs your heart, for a ſweet, pleaſant—— damn'd miſchievous ſon of a whore. [*Exeunt.*

ACT

ACT THE SECOND.

SCENE, an old-faſhioned Houſe.

Enter HARDCASTLE, followed by three or four aukward ſervants.

HARDCASTLE.

WELL, I hope you're perfect in the table exerciſe I have been teaching you theſe three days. You all know your poſts and your places, and can ſhew that you have been uſed to good company, without ever ſtirring from home.

OMNES.

Aye, aye.

HARDCASTLE.

When company comes, you are not to pop out and ſtare, and then run in again, like frighted rabbits in a warren.

OMNES.

No, no.

HARDCASTLE.

You, Diggory, whom I have taken from the barn, are to make a ſhew at the ſide-table; and you, Roger, whom I have advanced from the plough, are to place

place yourſelf behind my chair. But you're not to ſtand ſo, with your hands in your pockets. Take your hands from your pockets, Roger; and from your head, you blockhead you. See how Diggory carries his hands. They're a little too ſtiff, indeed, but that's no great matter.

DIGGORY.

Aye, mind how I hold them. I learned to hold my hands this way, when I was upon drill for the militia. And ſo being upon drill——

HARDCASTLE.

You muſt not be ſo talkative, Diggory. You muſt be all attention to the gueſts. You muſt hear us talk, and not think of talking; you muſt ſee us drink, and not think of drinking; you muſt ſee us eat, and not think of eating.

DIGGORY.

By the laws, your worſhip, that's parfectly unpoſſible. Whenever Diggory ſees yeating going forward, ecod he's always wiſhing for a mouthful himſelf.

HARDCASTLE.

Blockhead! Is not a belly-full in the kitchen as good as a belly-full in the parlour? Stay your ſtomach with that reflection.

DIGGORY.

Ecod I thank your worſhip, I'll make a ſhift to ſtay my ſtomach with a ſlice of cold beef in the pantry.

HARD-

HARDCASTLE.

Diggory, you are too talkative. Then if I happen to ſay a good thing, or tell a good ſtory at table, you muſt not all burſt out a-laughing, as if you made part of the company.

DIGGORY.

Then ecod your worſhip muſt not tell the ſtory of ould grouſe in the gun room: I can't help laughing at that—he! he! he!—for the ſoul of me. We have laughed at that theſe twenty years—ha! ha! ha!

HARDCASTLE.

Ha! ha! ha! The ſtory is a good one. Well, honeſt Diggory, you may laugh at that—but ſtill remember to be attentive.. Suppoſe one of the company ſhould call for a glaſs of wine, how will you behave? A glaſs of wine, Sir, if you pleaſe, (*To Diggory*)—Eh, why don't you move?

DIGGORY.

Ecod, your worſhip, I never have courage till I ſee the eatables and drinkables brought upo' the table, and then I'm as bauld as a lion.

HARDCASTLE.

What, will nobody move?

FIRST SERVANT.

I'm not to leave this place.

SECOND SERVANT.

I'm ſure it's no place of mine.

THIRD

THIRD SERVANT.

Nor mine, for ſartain.

DIGGORY.

Wauns, and I'm ſure it canna be mine.

HARDCASTLE.

You numbſkulls! and ſo while, like your betters, you are quarrelling for places, the gueſts muſt be ſtarved. O you dunces! I find I muſt begin all over again.——But don't I hear a coach drive into the yard? To your poſts, you blockheads. I'll go in the mean time and give my old friend's ſon a hearty reception at the gate. [*Exit* Hardcaſtle.

DIGGORY.

By the elevens, my place is gone quite out of my head.

ROGER.

I know that my place is to be every where.

FIRST SERVANT.

Where the devil is mine?

SECOND SERVANT.

My pleace is to be no where at all; and ſo ize go about my buſineſs. [*Exeunt ſervants, running about as if frighted, different ways.*

Enter SERVANT with Candles, ſhewing in MARLOW and HASTINGS.

SERVANT.

Welcome, gentlemen, very welcome! This way.

HAST-

HASTINGS.

After the disappointments of the day, welcome once more, Charles, to the comforts of a clean room and a good fire. Upon my word, a very well-looking house; antique but creditable.

MARLOW.

The usual fate of a large mansion. Having first ruined the master by good housekeeping, it at last comes to levy contributions as an inn.

HASTINGS.

As you say, we passengers are to be taxed to pay all these fineries. I have often seen a good side-board, or a marble chimney-piece, though not actually put in the bill, inflame a reckoning confoundedly.

MARLOW.

Travellers, George, must pay in all places. The only difference is, that in good inns, you pay dearly for luxuries; in bad inns, you are fleeced and starved.

HASTINGS.

You have lived pretty much among them. In truth, I have been often surprised, that you who have seen so much of the world, with your natural good sense, and your many opportunities, could never yet acquire a requisite share of assurance.

MARLOW.

The Englishman's malady. But tell me, George, where could I have learned that assurance you talk of? My life has been chiefly ſpent in a college, or an inn, in ſecluſion from that lovely part of the creation that chiefly teach men confidence. I don't know that I was ever familiarly acquainted with a ſingle modeſt woman—except my mother—But among females of another claſs you know—

HASTINGS.

Aye, among them you are impudent enough of all conſcience.

MARLOW.

They are of *us*, you know.

HASTINGS.

But in the company of women of reputation I never ſaw ſuch an idiot, ſuch a trembler; you look for all the world as if you wanted an opportunity of ſtealing out of the room.

MARLOW.

Why, man, that's becauſe I do want to ſteal out of the room. Faith, I have often formed a reſolution to break the ice, and rattle away at any rate. But I don't know how, a ſingle glance from a pair of fine eyes has totally overſet my reſolution. An impudent fellow may counterfeit modeſty, but I'll be hanged if a modeſt man can ever counterfeit impudence.

HASTINGS.

If you could but ſay half the fine things to them that I have heard you laviſh upon the bar-maid of an inn, or even a college bed-maker—

MAR-

MARLOW.

Why, George, I can't ſay fine things to them; they freeze, they petrify me. They may talk of a comet, or a burning mountain, or ſome ſuch bagatelle. But to me, a modeſt woman, dreſt out in all her finery, is the moſt tremendous object of the whole creation.

HASTINGS.

Ha! ha! ha! At this rate, man, how can you ever expect to marry?

MARLOW.

Never, unleſs, as among kings and princes, my bride were to be courted by proxy. If, indeed, like an eaſtern bridegroom, one were to be introduced to a wife he never ſaw before, it might be endured. But to go through all the terrors of a formal courtſhip, together with the epiſode of aunts, grandmothers, and couſins, and at laſt to blurt out the broad ſtaring queſtion of, madam, will you marry me? No, no, that's a ſtrain much above me, I aſſure you.

HASTINGS.

I pity you. But how do you intend behaving to the lady you are come down to viſit at the requeſt of your father?

MARLOW.

As I behave to all other ladies. Bow very low. Anſwer yes, or no, to all her demands—But for the reſt, I don't think I ſhall venture to look in her face, till I ſee my father's again.

HASTINGS.

I'm ſurpriſed that one who is ſo warm a friend can be ſo cool a lover.

MARLOW.

To be explicit, my dear Haſtings, my chief inducement down was to be inſtrumental in forwarding your happineſs, not my own. Miſs Neville loves you, the family don't know you, as my friend you are ſure of a reception, and let honour do the reſt.

HASTINGS.

My dear Marlow! But I'll ſuppreſs the emotion. Were I a wretch, meanly ſeeking to carry off a fortune, you ſhould be the laſt man in the world I would apply to for aſſiſtance. But Miſs Neville's perſon is all I aſk, and that is mine, both from her deceaſed father's conſent, and her own inclination.

MARLOW.

Happy man! You have talents and art to captivate any woman. I'm doom'd to adore the ſex, and yet to converſe with the only part of it I deſpiſe. This ſtammer in my addreſs, and this aukward prepoſſeſſing viſage of mine, can never permit me to ſoar above the reach of a milliner's 'prentice, or one of the ducheſſes of Drury-lane. Pſhaw! this fellow here to interrupt us.

Enter

Enter HARDCASTLE.

HARDCASTLE.

Gentlemen, once more you are heartily welcome. Which is Mr. Marlow? Sir, you're heartily welcome. It's not my way, you ſee, to receive my friends with my back to the fire. I like to give them a hearty reception in the old ſtyle at my gate. I like to ſee their horſes and trunks taken care of.

MARLOW (aſide.)

He has got our names from the ſervants already. (*To him*) We approve your caution and hoſpitality, Sir. (*To Haſtings*) I have been thinking, George, of changing our travelling dreſſes in the morning. I am grown confoundedly aſhamed of mine.

HARDCASTLE.

I beg, Mr. Marlow, you'll uſe no ceremony in this houſe.

HASTINGS.

I fancy, George, you're right: the firſt blow is half the battle. I intend opening the campaign with the white and gold.

HARDCASTLE.

Mr. Marlow—Mr. Haſtings—gentlemen—pray be under no conſtraint in this houſe. This is Liberty-hall, gentlemen. You may do juſt as you pleaſe here.

MARLOW.

Yet, George, if we open the campaign too fiercely at firſt, we may want ammunition before it is over. I think to reſerve the embroidery to ſecure a retreat.

HARDCASTLE.

Your talking of a retreat, Mr. Marlow, puts me in mind of the duke of Marlborough, when we went to beſiege Denain. He firſt ſummoned the garriſon.

MARLOW.

Don't you think the *ventre d'or* waiſtcoat will do with the plain brown?

HARDCASTLE.

He firſt ſummoned the garriſon, which might conſiſt of about five thouſand men——

HASTINGS.

I think not: brown and yellow mix but very poorly.

HARDCASTLE.

I ſay, gentlemen, as I was telling you, he ſummoned the garriſon, which might conſiſt of about five thouſand men——

MARLOW.

The girls like finery.

HARDCASTLE.

Which might conſiſt of about five thouſand men, well appointed with ſtores, ammunition, and other implements of war. Now, ſays the duke of Marlborough to George Brooks, that ſtood next to him —You muſt have heard of George Brooks—I'll pawn

pawn my dukedom, ſays he, but I take that garriſon without ſpilling a drop of blood. So——

MARLOW.

What, my good friend, if you gave us a glaſs of punch in the mean time, it would help us to carry on the ſiege with vigour.

HARDCASTLE.

Punch, Sir! (*Aſide*) This is the moſt unaccountable kind of modeſty I ever met with.

MARLOW.

Yes, Sir, punch. A glaſs of warm punch, after our journey, will be comfortable. This is Liberty-hall, you know.

HARDCASTLE.

Here's cup, Sir.

MARLOW.

(*Aſide*) So this fellow, in his Liberty-hall, will only let us have juſt what he pleaſes.

HARDCASTLE.

(*Taking the cup*) I hope you'll find it to your mind. I have prepared it with my own hands, and I believe you'll own the ingredients are tolerable. Will you be ſo good as to pledge me, Sir? Here, Mr. Marlow, here is to our better acquaintance.

(*Drinks.*)

MARLOW.

(*Aſide*) A very impudent fellow this! but he's a character and I'll humour him a little. Sir, my ſervice to you. (*Drinks.*)

HASTINGS.

(*Aſide*) I ſee this fellow wants to give us his company, and forgets that he's an innkeeper, before he has learned to be a gentleman.

MARLOW.

From the excellence of your cup, my old friend, I ſuppoſe you have a good deal of buſineſs in this part of the country. Warm work, now and then, at elections, I ſuppoſe.

HARDCASTLE.

No, Sir, I have long given that work over. Since our betters have hit upon the expedient of electing each other, there is no buſineſs 'for us that ſell ale.'

HASTINGS.

So, then you have no turn for politics I find.

HARDCASTLE.

Not in the leaſt. There was a time, indeed, I fretted myſelf about the miſtakes of government, like other people; but finding myſelf every day grow more angry, and the government growing no better, I left it to mend itſelf. Since that, I no more trouble my head about Heyder Ally or Ally Cawn, than about Ally Croaker. Sir, my ſervice to you.

HASTINGS.

So that with eating above ſtairs, and drinking below, with receiving your friends within, and amuſing them without, you lead a good pleaſant buſtling life of it.

HARD-

HARDCASTLE.

I do ſtir about a great deal, that's certain. Half the differences of the pariſh are adjuſted in this very parlour.

MARLOW.

(*After drinking*) And you have an argument in your cup, old gentleman, better than any in Weſtminſter-hall.

HARDCASTLE.

Aye, young gentleman, that, and a little philoſophy.

MARLOW.

(*Aſide.*) Well, this is the firſt time I ever heard of an innkeeper's philoſophy.

HASTINGS.

So then, like an experienced general, you attack them on every quarter. If you find their reaſon manageable, you attack it with your philoſophy; if you find they have no reaſon, you attack them with this. Here's your health, my philoſopher.

(*Drinks.*)

HARDCASTLE.

Good, very good, thank you; ha! ha! Your generalſhip puts me in mind of prince Eugene, when he fought the Turks at the battle of Belgrade. You ſhall hear.

MARLOW.

Inſtead of the battle of Belgrade, I believe it's almoſt time to talk about ſupper. What has your philoſophy got in the houſe for ſupper?

HARD-

HARDCASTLE.

For ſupper, Sir! (*Aſide*) Was ever ſuch a requeſt to a man in his own houſe!

MARLOW.

Yes, Sir, ſupper, Sir; I begin to feel an appetite. I ſhall make dev'liſh work to-night in the larder, I promiſe you.

HARDCASTLE.

(*Aſide*) Such a brazen dog ſure never my eyes beheld. (*To him*) Why really, Sir, as for ſupper I can't well tell. My Dorothy, and the cook-maid, ſettle theſe things between them. I leave theſe kind of things entirely to them.

MARLOW.

You do, do you?

HARDCASTLE.

Entirely. By-the-bye, I believe they are in actual conſultation upon what's for ſupper this moment in the kitchen.

MARLOW.

Then I beg they'll admit me as one of their privy council. It's a way I have got. When I travel, I always chuſe to regulate my own ſupper. Let the cook be called. No offence I hope, Sir.

HARDCASTLE.

O no, Sir, none in the leaſt; yet I don't know how: our Bridget, the cook-maid, is not very communicative upon theſe occaſions. Should we ſend for her, ſhe might ſcold us all out of the houſe.

HAST-

HASTINGS.

Let's ſee your liſt of the larder then. I aſk it as a favour. I always match my appetite to my bill of fare.

MARLOW.

(*To Hardcaſtle, who looks at them with ſurpriſe*) Sir, he's very right, and it's my way too.

HARDCASTLE.

Sir, you have a right to command here. Here, Roger, bring us the bill of fare for to-night's ſupper. I believe it's drawn out. Your manner, Mr. Haſtings, puts me in mind of my uncle, colonel Wallop. It was a ſaying of his, that no man was ſure of his ſupper till he had eaten it.

HASTINGS.

(*Aſide*) All upon the high ropes! His uncle a colonel! we ſhall ſoon hear of his mother being a juſtice of peace. But let's hear the bill of fare.

MARLOW.

(*Peruſing*) What's here? For the firſt courſe; for the ſecond courſe; for the deſert. The devil, Sir, do you think we have brought down the whole joiners company, or the corporation of Bedford, to eat up ſuch a ſupper? Two or three little things, clean and comfortable, will do.

HASTINGS.

But, let's hear it.

MARLOW.

(*Reading*) For the firſt courſe at the top, a pig, and pruin ſauce.

HASTINGS.

Damn your pig, I ſay.

MARLOW.

And damn your pruin ſauce, ſay I.

HARDCASTLE.

And yet, gentlemen, to men that are hungry, pig, with pruin ſauce, is very good eating.

MARLOW.

At the bottom, a calve's tongue and brains.

HASTINGS.

Let your brains be knock'd out, my good Sir; I don't like them.

MARLOW.

Or you may clap them on a plate by themſelves.

HARDCASTLE.

(*Aſide*) Their impudence confounds me. (*To them*) Gentlemen, you are my gueſts, make what alterations you pleaſe. Is there any thing elſe you wiſh to retrench or alter, gentlemen?

MARLOW.

Item. A pork pye, a boiled rabbit and ſauſages, a Florentine, a ſhaking pudding, and a diſh of tiff—taff—taffety cream!

HASTINGS.

Confound your made diſhes, I ſhall be as much at a loſs in this houſe as at a green and yellow din-

ner

ner at the French ambaſſador's table. I'm for plain eating.

HARDCASTLE.

I'm ſorry, gentlemen, that I have nothing you like, but if there be any thing you have a particular fancy to——

MARLOW.

Why, really, Sir, your bill of fare is ſo exquiſite, that any one part of it is full as good as another. Send us what you pleaſe. So much for ſupper. And now to ſee that our beds are air'd, and properly taken care of.

HARDCASTLE.

I entreat you'll leave all that to me. You ſhall not ſtir a ſtep.

MARLOW.

Leave that to you! I proteſt, Sir, you muſt excuſe me, I always look to theſe things myſelf.

HARDCASTLE.

I muſt inſiſt, Sir, you'll make yourſelf eaſy on that head.

MARLOW.

You ſee I'm reſolved on it. (*Aſide.*) A very troubleſome fellow this, as ever I met with.

HARDCASTLE.

Well, Sir, I'm reſolved at leaſt to attend you. (*Aſide*) This may be modern modeſty, but I never ſaw any thing look ſo like old-faſhioned impudence.

[*Exeunt* Marlow *and* Hardcaſtle.

HAST-

HASTINGS, ſolus.

So I find this fellow's civilities begin to grow troubleſome. But who can be angry at thoſe aſſiduities which are meant to pleaſe him? Ha! what do I ſee? Miſs Neville, by all that's happy!

Enter Miſs NEVILLE.

Miſs NEVILLE.

My dear Haſtings! To what unexpected good fortune? to what accident, am I to aſcribe this happy meeting?

HASTINGS.

Rather let me aſk the ſame queſtion, as I could never have hoped to meet my deareſt Conſtance at an inn.

Miſs NEVILLE.

An inn! ſure you miſtake! my aunt, my guardian, lives here. What could induce you to think this houſe an inn?

HASTINGS.

My friend, Mr. Marlow, with whom I came down, and I, have been ſent here as to an inn, I aſſure you. A young fellow whom we accidentally met at a houſe hard by directed us hither.

Miſs NEVILLE.

Certainly it muſt be one of my hopeful couſin's tricks, of whom you have heard me talk ſo often, ha! ha! ha!

HAST-

HASTINGS.

He whom your aunt intends for you? he of whom I have ſuch juſt apprehenſions?

Miſs NEVILLE.

You have nothing to fear from him, I aſſure you. You'd adore him if you knew how heartily he deſpiſes me. My aunt knows it too, and has undertaken to court me for him, and actually begins to think ſhe has made a conqueſt.

HASTINGS.

Thou dear diſſembler! You muſt know, my Conſtance, I have juſt ſeized this happy opportunity of my friend's viſit here to get admittance into the family. The horſes that carried us down are now fatigued with their journey, but they'll ſoon be refreſhed; and then, if my deareſt girl will truſt in her faithful Haſtings, we ſhall ſoon be landed in France, where even among ſlaves the laws of marriage are reſpected.

Miſs NEVILLE.

I have often told you, that, though ready to obey you, I yet ſhould leave my little fortune behind with reluctance. The greateſt part of it was left me by my uncle, the India director, and chiefly conſiſts in jewels. I have been for ſome time perſuading my aunt to let me wear them. I fancy I'm very near ſucceeding. The inſtant they are put into my poſſeſſion you ſhall find me ready to make them and myſelf yours.

HASTINGS.

Perish the baubles! Your person is all I desire. In the mean time, my friend Marlow must not be let into his mistake. I know the strange reserve of his temper is such, that if abruptly informed of it, he would instantly quit the house before our plan was ripe for execution.

Miss NEVILLE.

But how shall we keep him in the deception? Miss Hardcastle is just returned from walking; what if we still continue to deceive him?——This, this way—— [*They confer*.

Enter MARLOW.

MARLOW.

The affiduities of these good people teize me beyond bearing. My host seems to think it ill manners to leave me alone, and so he claps not only himself but his old-fashioned wife on my back. They talk of coming to sup with us too; and then, I suppose, we are to run the gauntlet through all the rest of the family.—What have we got here!—

HASTINGS.

My dear Charles! Let me congratulate you!— The most fortunate accident!—Who do you think is just alighted?

MARLOW.

Cannot guess.

HAST-

HASTINGS.

Our miſtreſſes, boy, Miſs Hardcaſtle and Miſs Neville. Give me leave to introduce Miſs Conſtance Neville to your acquaintance. Happening to dine in the neighbourhood, they called, on their return, to take freſh horſes here. Miſs Hardcaſtle has juſt ſtept into the next room, and will be back in an inſtant. Wasn't it lucky? eh!

MARLOW.

(*Aſide*) I have been mortified enough of all conſcience, and here comes ſomething to complete my embarraſſment.

HASTINGS.

Well! but was'nt it the moſt fortunate thing in the world?

MARLOW.

Oh! yes. Very fortunate—a moſt joyful encounter—But our dreſſes, George, you know are in diſorder—What if we ſhould poſtpone the happineſs 'till to-morrow?—To-morrow at her own houſe—It will be every bit as convenient—and rather more reſpectful—To-morrow let it be.

[*Offering to go.*

Miſs NEVILLE.

By no means, Sir. Your ceremony will diſpleaſe her. The diſorder of your dreſs will ſhew the ardour of your impatience. Beſides, ſhe knows you are in the houſe, and will permit you to ſee her.

MARLOW.

O! the devil! how ſhall I ſupport it? hem! hem! Haſtings, you muſt not go. You are to aſſiſt me, you know. I ſhall be confoundedly ridiculous. Yet, hang it! I'll take courage. Hem!

HASTINGS.

Pſhaw, man! it's but the firſt plunge, and all's over. She's but a woman, you know.

MARLOW.

And of all women, ſhe that I dread moſt to encounter!

Enter Miſs HARDCASTLE, as returned from walking, a bonnet, &c.

HASTINGS, introducing them.

Miſs Hardcaſtle, Mr. Marlow. I'm proud of bringing two perſons of ſuch merit together, that only want to know, to eſteem each other.

Miſs HARDCASTLE.

(*Aſide*) Now, for meeting my modeſt gentleman with a demure face, and quite in his own manner. (*After a pauſe, in which he appears very uneaſy and diſconcerted.*) I'm glad of your ſafe arrival, Sir— I'm told you had ſome accidents by the way.

MARLOW.

Only a few, madam. Yes, we had ſome. Yes, madam, a good many accidents, but ſhould be ſorry —madam—or rather glad of any accidents—that are ſo agreeably concluded. Hem!

HAST-

HASTINGS.

(*To him*) You never ſpoke better in your whole life. Keep it up, and I'll inſure you the victory.

Miſs HARDCASTLE.

I'm afraid you flatter, Sir. You that have ſeen ſo much of the fineſt company can find little entertainment in an obſcure corner of the country.

MARLOW.

(*Gathering courage*) I have lived, indeed, in the world, madam; but I have kept very little company. I have been but an obſerver upon life, madam, while others were enjoying it.

Miſs NEVILLE.

But that, I am told, is the way to enjoy it at laſt.

HASTINGS.

(*To him*) Cicero never ſpoke better. Once more, and you are confirmed in aſſurance for ever.

MARLOW.

(*To him*) Hem! ſtand by me then, and when I'm down, throw in a word or two to ſet me up again.

Miſs HARDCASTLE.

An obſerver, like you, upon life, were, I fear, diſagreeably employed, ſince you muſt have had much more to cenſure than to approve.

MARLOW.

Pardon me, madam. I was always willing to be amuſed. The folly of moſt people is rather an object of mirth than uneaſineſs.

HASTINGS.

(*To him*) Bravo, bravo. Never ſpoke ſo well in your whole life. Well! Miſs Hardcaſtle, I ſee that you and Mr. Marlow are going to be very good company. I believe our being here will but embarraſs the interview.

MARLOW.

Not in the leaſt, Mr. Haſtings. We like your company of all things. (*To him*) Zounds! George, ſure you won't go? how can you leave us?

HASTINGS.

Our preſence will but ſpoil converſation, ſo we'll retire to the next room. (*To him*) You don't conſider, man, that we are to manage a little tête-à-tête of our own. [*Exeunt.*

Miſs HARDCASTLE.

(*After a pauſe*) But you have not been wholly an obſerver, I preſume, Sir: the ladies I ſhould hope have employed ſome part of your addreſſes.

MARLOW.

(*Relapſing into timidity*) Pardon me, madam, I—I—I—as yet have ſtudied—only—to—deſerve them.

Miſs HARDCASTLE.

And that, ſome ſay, is the very worſt way to obtain them.

MARLOW.

Perhaps ſo, madam. But I love to converſe only with the more grave and ſenſible part of the ſex.—But I'm afraid I grow tireſome.

Miſs

Miſs Hardcastle.

Not at all, Sir; there is nothing I like ſo much as grave converſation myſelf; I could hear it for ever. Indeed I have often been ſurpriſed how a man of ſentiment could ever admire thoſe light airy pleaſures, where nothing reaches the heart.

Marlow.

It's——a diſeaſe——of the mind, madam. In the variety of taſtes there muſt be ſome who wanting a reliſh——for——um—a—um.

Miſs Hardcastle.

I underſtand you, Sir. There muſt be ſome, who wanting a reliſh for refined pleaſures, pretend to deſpiſe what they are incapable of taſting.

Marlow.

My meaning, madam, but infinitely better expreſſed. And I can't help obſerving——a——

Miſs Hardcastle.

(*Aſide*) Who could ever ſuppoſe this fellow impudent upon ſuch occaſions. (*To him*) You were going to obſerve, Sir——

Marlow.

I was obſerving, madam——I proteſt, madam, I forget what I was going to obſerve.

Miſs Hardcastle.

(*Aſide*) I vow and ſo do I. (*To him*) You were obſerving, Sir, that in this age of hypocriſy ſomething about hypocriſy, Sir.

MARLOW.

Yes, madam. In this age of hypocrisy there are few who upon strict inquiry do not—a—a—a——

Miss HARDCASTLE.

I understand you perfectly, Sir.

MARLOW.

(*Aside*) Egad! and that's more than I do myself.

Miss HARDCASTLE.

You mean that in this hypocritical age there are few that do not condemn in public what they practise in private, and think they pay every debt to virtue when they praise it.

MARLOW.

True, madam; those who have most virtue in their mouths, have least of it in their bosoms. But I'm sure I tire you, madam.

Miss HARDCASTLE.

Not in the least, Sir; there's something so agreeable and spirited in your manner, such life and force—pray, Sir, go on.

MARLOW.

Yes, madam. I was saying——that there are some occasions——when a total want of courage, madam, destroys all the——and puts us——upon a——a——a——

Miss HARDCASTLE.

I agree with you entirely, a want of courage upon some occasions assumes the appearance of ignorance, and

and betrays us when we moſt want to excel. I beg you'll proceed.

MARLOW.

Yes, madam. Morally ſpeaking, madam—But I ſee Miſs Neville expecting us in the next room. I would not intrude for the world.

Miſs HARDCASTLE.

I proteſt, Sir, I never was more agreeably entertained in all my life. Pray go on.

MARLOW.

Yes, madam. I was——But ſhe beckons us to join her. Madam, ſhall I do myſelf the honour to attend you?

Miſs HARDCASTLE.

Well then, I'll follow.

MARLOW.

(*Aſide*) This pretty ſmooth dialogue has done for me. [*Exit.*

Miſs HARDCASTLE, ſola.

Ha! ha! ha! Was there ever ſuch a ſober ſentimental interview? I'm certain he ſcarce look'd in my face the whole time. Yet the fellow, but for his unaccountable baſhfulneſs, is pretty well too. He has good ſenſe, but then ſo buried in his fears, that it fatigues one more than ignorance. If I could teach him a little confidence, it would be doing ſomebody that I know of a piece of ſervice. But who is that ſomebody?—That, faith, is a queſtion I can ſcarce anſwer. [*Exit.*

Enter TONY and Miſs NEVILLE, followed by Mrs. HARDCASTLE and HASTINGS.

TONY.

What do you follow me for, couſin Con? I wonder you're not aſham'd to be ſo very engaging.

Miſs NEVILLE.

I hope, couſin, one may ſpeak to one's own relations, and not be to blame.

TONY.

Aye, but I know what ſort of a relation you want to make me though; but it won't do. I tell you, couſin Con, it won't do; ſo I beg you'll keep your diſtance, I want no nearer relationſhip.

[*She follows, coquetting him to the back ſcene.*

Mrs. HARDCASTLE.

Well! I vow, Mr. Haſtings, you are very entertaining. There's nothing in the world I love to talk of ſo much as London, and the faſhions, though I was never there myſelf.

HASTINGS.

Never there! You amaze me! From your air and manner, I conclude you had been bred all your life either at Ranelagh, St. James's, or Tower Wharf.

Mrs. HARDCASTLE.

O! Sir, you're only pleaſed to ſay ſo. We country perſons can have no manner at all. I'm in love with the town, and that ſerves to raiſe me

above

above ſome of our neighbouring ruſtics; but who can have a manner, that has never ſeen the Pantheon, the Grotto Gardens, the Borough, and ſuch places where the nobility chiefly reſort? All I can do, is to enjoy London at ſecond-hand. I take care to know every tête-à-tête from the ſcandalous magazine, and have all the faſhions, as they come out, in a letter from the two Miſs Rickets of Crooked-lane. Pray how do you like this head, Mr. Haſtings?

HASTINGS.

Extremely elegant and degagée, upon my word, madam. Your friſeur is a Frenchman, I ſuppoſe?

Mrs. HARDCASTLE.

I proteſt I dreſſed it myſelf from a print in the ladies memorandum-book for the laſt year.

HASTINGS.

Indeed! Such a head in a ſide-box, at the playhouſe, would draw as many gazers as my lady may'reſs at a city ball.

Mrs. HARDCASTLE.

I vow, ſince inoculation began, there is no ſuch thing to be ſeen as a plain woman; ſo one muſt dreſs a little particular, or one may eſcape in the crowd.

HASTINGS.

But that can never be your caſe, madam, in any dreſs. (*Bowing.*)

Mrs.

Mrs. Hardcastle.

Yet, what ſignifies my dreſſing when I have ſuch a piece of antiquity by my ſide as Mr. Hardcaſtle: all I can ſay will never argue down a ſingle button from his cloaths. I have often wanted him to throw off his great flaxen wig, and where he was bald, to plaiſter it over, like my Lord Pately, with powder.

Hastings.

You are right, madam; for, as among the ladies there are none ugly, ſo among the men there are none old.

Mrs. Hardcastle.

But what do you think his anſwer was? Why, with his uſual Gothic vivacity, he ſaid I only wanted him to throw off his wig to convert it into a tête for my own wearing.

Hastings.

Intolerable! At your age you may wear what you pleaſe, and it muſt become you.

Mrs. Hardcastle.

Pray, Mr. Haſtings, what do you take to be the moſt faſhionable age about town?

Hastings.

Some time ago, forty was all the mode; but I'm told the ladies intend to bring up fifty for the enſuing winter.

Mrs. Hardcastle.

Seriouſly. Then I ſhall be too young for the faſhion.

Hast-

HASTINGS.

No lady begins now to put on jewels 'till ſhe's paſt forty. For inſtance, Miſs there, in a polite circle, would be conſidered as a child, as a mere maker of ſamplers.

Mrs. HARDCASTLE.

And yet Mrs. Niece thinks herſelf as much a woman, and is as fond of jewels as the oldeſt of us all.

HASTINGS.

Your niece, is ſhe? And that young gentleman, a brother of yours, I ſhould preſume?

Mrs. HARDCASTLE.

My ſon, Sir. They are contracted to each other. Obſerve their little ſports. They fall in and out ten times a day, as if they were man and wife already. (*To them*) Well, Tony, child, what ſoft things are you ſaying to your couſin Conſtance this evening?

TONY.

I have been ſaying no ſoft things; but that it's very hard to be followed about ſo. Ecod! I've not a place in the houſe now that's left to myſelf, but the ſtable.

Mrs. HARDCASTLE.

Never mind him, Con, my dear. He's in another ſtory behind your back.

Miſs

Miſs NEVILLE.

There's ſomething generous in my couſin's manner. He falls out before faces to be forgiven in private.

TONY.

That's a damned confounded—crack.

Mrs. HARDCASTLE.

Ah! he's a ſly one. Don't you think they're like each other about the mouth, Mr. Haſtings? The Blenkinſop mouth to a T. They're of a ſize too. Back to back, my pretties, that Mr. Haſtings may ſee you. Come, Tony.

TONY.

You had as good not make me, I tell you.

(*Meaſuring.*)

Miſs NEVILLE.

O lud! he has almoſt cracked my head.

Mrs. HARDCASTLE.

O the monſter! For ſhame, Tony. You a man, and behave ſo!

TONY.

If I'm a man, let me have my fortin. Ecod! I'll not be made a fool of no longer.

Mrs. HARDCASTLE.

Is this, ungrateful boy, all that I'm to get for the pains I have taken in your education? I that have rock'd you in your cradle, and fed that pretty mouth with a ſpoon! Did not I work that waiſtcoat to make you genteel? Did not I preſcribe for

you

you every day, and weep while the receipt was operating?

TONY.

Ecod! you had reaſon to weep, for you have been doſing me ever ſince I was born. I have gone through every receipt in the complete houſewife ten times over; and you have thoughts of courſing me through Quincy next ſpring. But, ecod! I tell you, I'll not be made a fool of no longer.

Mrs. HARDCASTLE.

Wasn't it all for your good, viper? Wasn't it all for your good?

TONY.

I wiſh you'd let me and my good alone then. Snubbing this way when I'm in ſpirits. If I'm to have any good, let it come of itſelf; not to keep dinging it, dinging it into one ſo.

Mrs. HARDCASTLE.

That's falſe; I never ſee you when you're in ſpirits. No, Tony, you then go to the alehouſe or kennel. I'm never to be delighted with your agreeable, wild notes, unfeeling monſter!

TONY.

Ecod! mamma, your own notes are the wildeſt of the two.

Mrs. HARDCASTLE.

Was ever the like? But I ſee he wants to break my heart, I ſee he does.

HAST.

HASTINGS.

Dear madam, permit me to lecture the young gentleman a little. I'm certain I can perſuade him to his duty.

Mrs. HARDCASTLE.

Well! I muſt retire. Come, Conſtance, my love. You ſee, Mr. Haſtings, the wretchedneſs of my ſituation: was ever poor woman ſo plagued with a dear, ſweet, pretty, provoking, undutiful boy. [*Exeunt* Mrs. Hardcaſtle *and* Miſs Neville.

HASTINGS, TONY.

TONY, ſinging.

" There was a young man riding by, and fain " would have his will. Rang do didlo dee."—— Don't mind her. Let her cry. It's the comfort of her heart. I have ſeen her and ſiſter cry over a book for an hour together, and they ſaid, they liked the book the better the more it made them cry.

HASTINGS.

Then you're no friend to the ladies, I find, my pretty young gentleman?

TONY.

That's as I find 'um.

HASTINGS.

Not to her of your mother's chuſing, I dare anſwer? And yet ſhe appears to me a pretty well-tempered girl.

TONY.

TONY.

That's becauſe you don't know her as well as I. Ecod! I know every inch about her; and there's not a more bitter cantanckerous toad in all chriſtendom.

HASTINGS.

(*Aſide*) Pretty encouragement this for a lover!

TONY.

I have ſeen her ſince the height of that. She has as many tricks as a hare in a thicket, or a colt the firſt day's breaking.

HASTINGS.

To me ſhe appears ſenſible and ſilent!

TONY.

Aye, before company. But when ſhe's with her play-mate ſhe's as loud as a hog in a gate.

HASTINGS.

But there is a meek modeſty about her that charms me.

TONY.

Yes, but curb her never ſo little, ſhe kicks up, and you're flung in a ditch.

HASTINGS.

Well, but you muſt allow her a little beauty.—Yes, you muſt allow her ſome beauty.

TONY.

Bandbox! She's all a made up thing, mum. Ah! could you but ſee Bet Bouncer of theſe parts, you

you might then talk of beauty. Ecod, ſhe has two eyes as black as ſloes, and cheeks as broad and red as a pulpit cuſhion. She'd make two of ſhe.

HASTINGS.

Well, what ſay you to a friend that would take this bitter bargain off your hands?

TONY.

Anon.

HASTINGS.

Would you thank him that would take Miſs Neville, and leave you to happineſs and your dear Betſy?

TONY.

Aye; but where is there ſuch a friend, for who would take her?

HASTINGS.

I am he. If you but aſſiſt me, I'll engage to whip her off to France, and you ſhall never hear more of her.

TONY.

Aſſiſt you! Ecod I will, to the laſt drop of my blood. I'll clap a pair of horſes to your chaiſe that ſhall trundle you off in a twinkling, and may be get you a part of her fortin beſide, in jewels, that you little dream of.

HASTINGS.

My dear 'ſquire, this looks like a lad of ſpirit.

TONY.

TONY.

Come along then, and you ſhall ſee more of my ſpirit before you have done with me. (*Singing.*)

We are the boys
That fears no noiſe
Where the thundering cannons roar.

[*Exeunt.*

ACT THE THIRD.

Enter HARDCASTLE, ſolus.

HARDCASTLE.

WHAT could my old friend Sir Charles mean by recommending his ſon as the modeſteſt young man in town? To me he appears the moſt impudent piece of braſs that ever ſpoke with a tongue. He has taken poſſeſſion of the eaſy chair by the fire-ſide already. He took off his boots in the parlour, and deſired me to ſee them taken care of. I'm deſirous to know how his impudence affects my daughter.—She will certainly be ſhocked at it.

Enter Miſs HARDCASTLE, plainly dreſſed.

HARDCASTLE.

Well, my Kate, I ſee you have changed your dreſs as I bid you; and yet, I believe, there was no great occaſion.

Miſs HARDCASTLE.

I find ſuch a pleaſure, Sir, in obeying your commands, that I take care to obſerve them without ever debating their propriety.

HARD-

HARDCASTLE.

And yet, Kate, I ſometimes give you ſome cauſe, particularly when I recommended my modeſt gentleman to you as a lover to-day.

Miſs HARDCASTLE.

You taught me to expect ſomething extraordinary, and I find the original exceeds the deſcription.

HARDCASTLE.

I was never ſo ſurpriſed in my life! He has quite confounded all my faculties!

Miſs HARDCASTLE.

I never ſaw any thing like it: and a man of the world too!

HARDCASTLE.

Aye, he learned it all abroad,—what a fool was I, to think a young man could learn modeſty by travelling. He might as ſoon learn wit at a maſquerade.

Miſs HARDCASTLE.

It ſeems all natural to him.

HARDCASTLE.

A good deal aſſiſted by bad company and a French dancing-maſter.

Miſs HARDCASTLE.

Sure you miſtake, papa! A French dancing-maſter could never have taught him that timid look, —that aukward addreſs,—that baſhful manner—

HARDCASTLE.

Whoſe look? whoſe manner, child?

Miss Hardcastle.

Mr. Marlow's: his *mauvaise honte*, his timidity struck me at the first sight.

Hardcastle.

Then your first sight deceived you; for I think him one of the most brazen first sights that ever astonished my senses.

Miss Hardcastle.

Sure, Sir, you rally! I never saw any one so modest.

Hardcastle.

And can you be serious! I never saw such a bouncing swaggering puppy since I was born. Bully Dawson was but a fool to him.

Miss Hardcastle.

Surprising! He met me with a respectful bow, a stammering voice, and a look fixed on the ground.

Hardcastle.

He met me with a loud voice, a lordly air, and a familiarity that made my blood freeze again.

Miss Hardcastle.

He treated me with diffidence and respect; censured the manners of the age; admired the prudence of girls that never laughed; tired me with apologies for being tiresome; then left the room with a bow, and, "madam, I would not for the "world detain you."

Hardcastle.

He spoke to me as if he knew me all his life before. Asked twenty questions, and never waited

for

for an anſwer, interrupted my beſt remarks with ſome ſilly pun, and when I was in my beſt ſtory of the Duke of Marlborough and Prince Eugene, he aſked if I had not a good hand at making punch. Yes, Kate, he aſked your father if he was a maker of punch.

Miſs HARDCASTLE.

One of us muſt certainly be miſtaken.

HARDCASTLE.

If he be what he he has ſhewn himſelf, I'm determined he ſhall never have my conſent.

Miſs HARDCASTLE.

And if he be the ſullen thing I take him, he ſhall never have mine.

HARDCASTLE.

In one thing then we are agreed—to reject him.

Miſs HARDCASTLE.

Yes. But upon conditions. For if you ſhould find him leſs impudent, and I more preſuming; if you find him more reſpectful, and I more importunate——I don't know——the fellow is well enough for a man—Certainly we don't meet many ſuch at a horſe race in the country.

HARDCASTLE.

If we ſhould find him ſo——But that's impoſſible. The firſt appearance has done my buſineſs. I'm ſeldom deceived in that.

Miſs HARDCASTLE.

And yet there may be many good qualities under that firſt appearance.

HARDCASTLE.

Aye, when a girl finds a fellow's outſide to her taſte, ſhe then ſets about gueſſing the reſt of his furniture. With her, a ſmooth face ſtands for good ſenſe, and a genteel figure for every virtue.

Miſs HARDCASTLE.

I hope, Sir, a converſation begun with a compliment to my good ſenſe won't end with a ſneer at my underſtanding?

HARDCASTLE.

Pardon me, Kate. But if young Mr. Brazen can find the art of reconciling contradictions, he may pleaſe us both, perhaps.

Miſs HARDCASTLE.

And as one of us muſt be miſtaken, what if we go to make further diſcoveries?

HARDCASTLE.

Agreed. But depend on't I'm in the right.

Miſs HARDCASTLE.

And depend on't I'm not much in the wrong.

[*Exeunt.*

Enter TONY, running in with a caſket.

TONY.

Ecod! I have got them. Here they are. My couſin Con's necklaces, bobs and all. My mother ſhan't cheat the poor ſouls out of their fortin neither. O! my genus, is that you?

Enter

Enter HASTINGS.

HASTINGS.

My dear friend, how have you managed with your mother? I hope you have amufed her with pretending love for your coufin, and that you are willing to be reconciled at laft? Our horfes will be refrefhed in a fhort time, and we fhall foon be ready to fet off.

TONY.

And here's fomething to bear your charges by the way, (*giving the cafket*) your fweetheart's jewels. Keep them, and hang thofe, I fay, that would rob you of one of them.

HASTINGS.

But how have you procured them from your mother?

TONY.

Afk me no queftions, and I'll tell you no fibs. I procured them by the rule of thumb. If I had not a key to every drawer in mother's bureau, how could I go to the alehoufe fo often as I do? An honeft man may rob himfelf of his own at any time.

HASTINGS.

Thoufands do it every day. But to be plain with you, Mifs Neville is endeavouring to procure them from her aunt this very inftant. If fhe fucceeds, it will be the moft delicate way at leaft of obtaining them.

TONY.

Well, keep them, till you know how it will be, But I know how it will be well enough, ſhe'd as ſoon part with the only ſound tooth in her head.

HASTINGS.

But I dread the effects of her reſentment, when ſhe finds ſhe has loſt them.

TONY.

Never you mind her reſentment, leave me to manage that. I don't value her reſentment the bounce of a cracker. Zounds! here they are. Morrice! Prance! [*Exit* Haſtings.

TONY, Mrs. HARDCASTLE, and Miſs NEVILLE.

Mrs. HARDCASTLE.

Indeed, Conſtance, you amaze me. Such a girl as you want jewels? It will be time enough for jewels, my dear, twenty years hence, when your beauty begins to want repairs.

Miſs NEVILLE.

But what will repair beauty at forty, will certainly improve it at twenty, madam.

Mrs. HARDCASTLE.

Yours, my dear, can admit of none. That natural bluſh is beyond a thouſand ornaments. Beſides, child, jewels are quite out at preſent. Don't you ſee half the ladies of our acquaintance, my lady Kill-day-light, and Mrs. Crump, and the reſt of them,

them, carry their jewels to town, and bring nothing but paſte and marcaſites back.

Miſs NEVILLE.

But who knows, madam, but ſomebody that ſhall be nameleſs would like me beſt with all my little finery about me?

Mrs. HARDCASTLE.

Conſult your glaſs, my dear, and then ſee if, with ſuch a pair of eyes, you want any better ſparklers. What do you think, Tony, my dear? does your couſin Con, want any jewels, in your eyes, to ſet off her beauty?

TONY.

That's as thereafter may be.

Miſs NEVILLE.

My dear aunt, if you knew how it would oblige me.

Mrs. HARDCASTLE.

A parcel of old-faſhioned roſe and table cut things. They would make you look like the court of king Solomon at a puppet-ſhew. Beſides, I believe I can't readily come at them. They may be miſſing for aught I know to the contrary.

TONY.

(*Apart to Mrs. Hardcaſtle.*) Then why don't you tell her ſo at once, as ſhe's ſo longing for them? Tell her they're loſt. It's the only way to quiet her. Say they're loſt, and call me to bear witneſs.

Mrs.

Mrs. Hardcastle.

(*Apart to Tony.*) You know, my dear, I'm only keeping them for you. So if I ſay they're gone, you'll bear me witneſs, will you? He! he! he!

Tony.

Never fear me. Ecod! I'll ſay I ſaw them taken out with my own eyes.

Miſs Neville.

I deſire them but for a day, madam. Juſt to be permitted to ſhew them as relics, and then they may be lock'd up again.

Mrs. Hardcastle.

To be plain with you, my dear Conſtance; if I could find them, you ſhould have them. They're miſſing, I aſſure you. Loſt, for aught I know; but we muſt have patience wherever they are.

Miſs Neville.

I'll not believe it; this is but a ſhallow pretence to deny me. I know they're too valuable to be ſo ſlightly kept, and as you are to anſwer for the loſs.

Mrs. Hardcastle.

Don't be alarm'd, Conſtance. If they be loſt, I muſt reſtore an equivalent. But my ſon knows they are miſſing, and not to be found.

Tony.

That I can bear witneſs to. They are miſſing, and not to be found, I'll take my oath on't.

Mrs.

Mrs. HARDCASTLE.

You must learn resignation, my dear; for though we lose our fortune, yet we should not lose our patience. See me, how calm I am.

Miss NEVILLE.

Aye, people are generally calm at the misfortunes of others.

Mrs. HARDCASTLE.

Now, I wonder a girl of your good sense should waste a thought upon such trumpery. We shall soon find them; and, in the mean time, you shall make use of my garnets till your jewels be found.

Miss NEVILLE.

I detest garnets.

Mrs. HARDCASTLE.

The most becoming things in the world to set off a clear complexion. You have often seen how well they look upon me, You shall have them. [*Exit.*

Miss NEVILLE.

I dislike them of all things. You shan't stir.—Was ever any thing so provoking to mislay my own jewels, and force me to wear her trumpery.

TONY.

Don't be a fool. If she gives you the garnets, take what you can get. The jewels are your own already. I have stolen them out of her bureau, and she does not know it. Fly to your spark, he'll tell you more of the matter. Leave me to manage her.

Miss NEVILLE.

My dear cousin!

TONY.

TONY.

Vanifh. She's here, and has miffed them already. Zounds! how fhe fidgets and fpits about like a catharine wheel.

Enter Mrs. HARDCASTLE.

Mrs. HARDCASTLE.

Confufion! thieves! robbers! we are cheated, plundered, broke open, undone.

TONY.

What's the matter, what's the matter, mamma? I hope nothing has happened to any of the good family!

Mrs. HARDCASTLE.

We are robbed. My bureau has been broke open, the jewels taken out, and I'm undone.

TONY.

Oh! is that all? Ha! ha! ha! By the laws, I never faw it better acted in my life. Ecod, I thought you was ruin'd in earneft, ha! ha! ha!

Mrs. HARDCASTLE.

Why, boy, I'm ruin'd in earneft. My bureau has been broke open, and all taken away.

TONY.

Stick to that; ha! ha! ha! ftick to that. I'll bear witnefs, you know, call me to bear witnefs.

Mrs. HARDCASTLE.

I tell you, Tony, by all that's precious, the jewels are gone, and I fhall be ruin'd for ever.

TONY.

TONY.

Sure I know they're gone, and I'm to ſay ſo.

Mrs. HARDCASTLE.

My deareſt Tony, but hear me. They're gone, I ſay.

TONY.

By the laws, mamma, you make me for to laugh, ha! ha! I know who took them, well enough, ha! ha! ha!

Mrs. HARDCASTLE.

Was there ever ſuch a blockhead, that can't tell the difference between jeſt and earneſt? I tell you I'm not in jeſt, booby.

TONY.

That's right, that's right: you muſt be in a bitter paſſion, and then nobody will ſuſpect either of us. I'll bear witneſs that they are gone.

Mrs. HARDCASTLE.

Was there ever ſuch a croſs-grain'd brute, that won't hear me? Can you bear witneſs that you're no better than a fool? Was ever poor woman ſo beſet with fools on one hand, and thieves on the other.

TONY.

I can bear witneſs to that.

Mrs. HARDCASTLE.

Bear witneſs again, you blockhead you, and I'll turn you out of the room directly. My poor niece, what will become of her! Do you laugh, you unfeeling brute, as if you enjoyed my diſtreſs?

TONY.

TONY.

I can bear witneſs to that.

Mrs. HARDCASTLE.

Do you inſult me, monſter? I'll teach you to vex your mother, I will.

TONY.

I can bear witneſs to that.

[*He runs off, ſhe follows him.*

Enter Miſs HARDCASTLE and Maid.

Miſs HARDCASTLE.

What an unaccountable creature is that brother of mine, to ſend them to the houſe as an inn, ha! ha! I don't wonder at his impudence.

MAID.

But what is more, madam, the young gentleman, as you paſſed by in your preſent dreſs, aſk'd me if you were the bar-maid? He miſtook you for the bar-maid, madam.

Miſs HARDCASTLE.

Did he? Then as I live, I'm reſolved to keep up the deluſion. Tell me, Pimple, how do you like my preſent dreſs. Don't you think I look ſomething like Cherry in the Beaux Stratagem?

MAID.

It's the dreſs, madam, that every lady wears in the country, but when ſhe viſits, or receives company.

Miſs

Miſs HARDCASTLE.

And are you ſure he does not remember my face or perſon?

MAID.

Certain of it.

Miſs HARDCASTLE.

I vow, I thought ſo? for though we ſpoke for ſome time together, yet his fears were ſuch, that he never once looked up during the interview. Indeed, if he had, my bonnet would have kept him from ſeeing me.

MAID.

But what do you hope from keeping him in his miſtake?

Miſs HARDCASTLE.

In the firſt place, I ſhall be ſeen, and that is no ſmall advantage to a girl who brings her face to market. Then I ſhall perhaps make an acquaintance, and that's no ſmall victory gained over one who never addreſſes any but the wildeſt of her ſex. But my chief aim is to take my gentleman off his guard, and, like an inviſible champion of romance, examine the giant's force before I offer to combat.

MAID.

But are you ſure you can act your part, and diſguiſe your voice, ſo that he may miſtake that, as he has already miſtaken your perſon?

Miſs HARDCASTLE.

Never fear me. I think I have got the true barcant.—Did your honour call?——Attend the Lion there.—

there.—Pipes and tobacco for the Angel.—The Lamb has been outrageous this half hour.

MAID.

It will do, madam. But he's here. [*Exit* Maid.

Enter MARLOW.

MARLOW.

What a bawling in every part of the houſe! I have ſcarce a moment's repoſe. If I go to the beſt room, there I find my hoſt and his ſtory. If I fly to the gallery, there we have my hoſteſs with her courteſy down to the ground. I have at laſt got a moment to myſelf, and now for recollection.

[*Walks and muſes.*

Miſs HARDCASTLE.

Did you call, Sir? Did your honour call?

MARLOW.

(*Muſing.*) As for Miſs Hardcaſtle, ſhe's too grave and ſentimental for me.

Miſs HARDCASTLE.

Did your honour call?

[*She ſtill places herſelf before him, he turning away.*

MARLOW.

No, child, (*muſing.*) Beſides, from the glimpſe I had of her, I think ſhe ſquints.

Miſs HARDCASTLE.

I'm ſure, Sir, I heard the bell ring.

MAR-

MARLOW.

No, no. (*musing.*) I have pleased my father, however, by coming down, and I'll to-morrow please myself by returning.

(*Taking out his tablets, and perusing.*

Miss HARDCASTLE.

Perhaps the other gentleman called, Sir?

MARLOW.

I tell you, no.

Miss HARDCASTLE.

I should be glad to know, Sir. We have such a parcel of servants.

MARLOW.

No, no, I tell you. (*Looks full in her face*). Yes, child, I think I did call. I wanted—I wanted——I vow, child, you are vastly handsome.

Miss HARDCASTLE.

O la, Sir, you'll make one asham'd.

MARLOW.

Never saw a more sprightly malicious eye. Yes, yes, my dear, I did call. Have you got any of your —a—what d'ye call it in the house?

Miss HARDCASTLE.

No, Sir, we have been out of that these ten days.

MARLOW.

One may call in this house, I find, to very little purpose. Suppose I should call for a taste, just by way of trial, of the nectar of your lips; perhaps I might be disappointed in that too.

Miſs HARDCASTLE.

Nectar! nectar! That's a liquor there's no call for in thoſe parts. French, I ſuppoſe. We keep no French wines here, Sir.

MARLOW.

Of true Engliſh growth, I aſſure you.

Miſs HARDCASTLE.

Then it's odd I ſhould not know it. We brew all ſorts of wines in this houſe, and I have lived here theſe eighteen years.

MARLOW.

Eighteen years! Why one would think, child, you kept the bar before you were born. How old are you?

Miſs HARDCASTLE.

O! Sir, I muſt not tell my age. They ſay women and muſic ſhould never be dated.

MARLOW.

To gueſs at this diſtance you can't be much above forty (*approaching*). Yet nearer I don't think ſo much (*approaching*). By coming cloſe to ſome women they look younger ſtill; but when we come very cloſe indeed—(*attempting to kiſs her*).

Miſs HARDCASTLE.

Pray, Sir, keep your diſtance. One would think you wanted to know one's age as they do horſes, by mark of mouth.

MAR-

MARLOW.

I protest, child, you use me extremely ill. If you keep me at this distance, how is it possible you and I can ever be acquainted?

Miss HARDCASTLE.

And who wants to be acquainted with you? I want no such acquaintance, not I. I'm sure you did not treat Miss Hardcastle that was here awhile ago in this obstropalous manner. I'll warrant me, before her you look'd dash'd, and kept bowing to the ground, and talk'd, for all the word, as if you was before a justice of peace.

MARLOW.

(*Aside*) Egad! She has hit it, sure enough. (*To her*) In awe of her, child? Ha! ha! ha! A mere, aukward, squinting thing, no, no. I find you don't know me. I laugh'd, and rallied her a little; but I was unwilling to be too severe. No, I could not be too severe, curse me!

Miss HARDCASTLE.

O! then, Sir, you are a favourite, I find, among the ladies?

MARLOW.

Yes, my dear, a great favourite. And yet, hang me, I don't see what they find in me to follow. At the ladies club in town, I'm called their agreeable Rattle. Rattle, child, is not my real name, but one I'm known by. My name is Solomons. Mr.

P 2 Solo-

Solomons, my dear, at your ſervice. (*Offering to ſalute her.*)

Miſs Hardcastle.

Hold, Sir; you are introducing me to your club, not to yourſelf. And you're ſo great a favourite there, you ſay?

Marlow.

Yes, my dear. There's Mrs. Mantrap, lady Betty Blackleg, theounteſs of Sligo, Mrs. Langhorns, old Miſs Biddy Buckſkin, and your humble ſervant, keep up the ſpirit of the place.

Miſs Hardcastle.

Then it's a very merry place, I ſuppoſe?

Marlow.

Yes, as merry as cards, ſupper, wine, and old women, can make us.

Miſs Hardcastle.

And their agreeable Rattle, ha! ha! ha!

Marlow.

(*Aſide*) Egad! I don't quite like this chit. She looks knowing, methinks. You laugh, child!

Miſs Hardcastle.

I can't but laugh to think what time they all have for minding their work or their family.

Marlow.

(*Aſide*) All's well; ſhe don't laugh at me. (*To her*) Do you ever work, child?

Miſs

Miſs HARDCASTLE.

Aye, ſure. There's not a ſcreen or a quilt in the whole houſe but what can bear witneſs to that.

MARLOW.

Odſo! then you muſt ſhew me your embroidery. I embroider and draw patterns myſelf a little. If you want a judge of your work you muſt apply to me. [*Seizing her hand.*

Miſs HARDCASTLE.

Aye, but the colours do not look well by candle-light. You ſhall ſee all in the morning.

[*Struggling.*

MARLOW.

And why not now, my angel? Such beauty fires beyond the power of reſiſtance.——Pſhaw! the father here! My old luck: I never nick'd ſeven that I did not throw ames ace three times following.

[*Exit* Marlow.

Enter HARDCASTLE, who ſtands in ſurprize.

HARDCASTLE.

So, madam. So I find this is your modeſt lover. This is your humble admirer that kept his eyes fixed on the ground, and only ador'd at humble diſtance. Kate, Kate, art thou not aſham'd to deceive your father ſo?

Miſs HARDCASTLE.

Never truſt me, dear papa, but he's ſtill the modeſt man I firſt took him for, you'll be convinc'd of it as well as I.

HARDCASTLE.

By the hand of my body I believe his impudence is infectious! Didn't I ſee him ſeize your hand? Didn't I ſee him hawl you about like a milk-maid? and now you talk of his reſpect and his modeſty, forſooth!

Miſs HARDCASTLE.

But if I ſhortly convince you of his modeſty, that he has only the faults that will paſs off with time, and the virtues that will improve with age, I hope you'll forgive him.

HARDCASTLE.

The girl would actually make one run mad! I tell you I'll not be convinced. I am convinced. He has ſcarce been three hours in the houſe, and he has already encroached on all my prerogatives. You may like his impudence, and call it modeſty. But my ſon-in-law, madam, muſt have very different qualifications.

Miſs HARDCASTLE.

Sir, I aſk but this night to convince you.

HARDCASTLE.

You ſhall not have half the time, for I have thoughts of turning him out this very hour.

Miſs HARDCASTLE.

Give me that hour then, and I hope to ſatisfy you.

HARDCASTLE.

Well, an hour let it be then. But I'll have no trifling with your father. All fair and open, do you mind me.

Miſs HARDCASTLE.

I hope, Sir, you have ever found that I conſidered your commands as my pride; for your kindneſs is ſuch, that my duty as yet has been inclination.

ACT THE FOURTH.

Enter Hastings and Miſs Neville.

Hastings.

You ſurpriſe me! Sir Charles Marlow expected here this night? Where have you had your information?

Miſs Neville.

You may depend upon it. I juſt ſaw his letter to Mr. Hardcaſtle, in which he tells him he intends ſetting out a few hours after his ſon.

Hastings.

Then, my Conſtance, all muſt be compleated before he arrives. He knows me; and ſhould he find me here, would diſcover my name, and perhaps my deſigns, to the reſt of the family.

Miſs Neville.

The jewels, I hope, are ſafe.

Hastings.

Yes, yes. I have ſent them to Marlow, who keeps the keys of our baggage. In the mean time, I'll go to prepare matters for our elopement. I have had the 'ſquire's promiſe of a freſh pair of horſes;

and,

and, if I ſhould not ſee him again, will write him further directions. [*Exit.*

Miſs NEVILLE.

Well! ſucceſs attend you. In the mean time, I'll go amuſe my aunt with the old pretence of a violent paſſion for my couſin. [*Exit.*

Enter MARLOW, followed by a ſervant.

MARLOW.

I wonder what Haſtings could mean by ſending me ſo valuable a thing as a caſket to keep for him, when he knows the only place I have is the ſeat of a poſt-coach at an inn-door. Have you depoſited the caſket with the landlady, as I ordered you? Have you put it into her own hands?

SERVANT.

Yes, your honour.

MARLOW.

She ſaid ſhe'd keep it ſafe, did ſhe?

SERVANT.

Yes, ſhe ſaid ſhe'd keep it ſafe enough; ſhe aſk'd me how I came by it? and ſhe ſaid ſhe had a great mind to make me give an account of myſelf.

[*Exit* Servant.

MARLOW.

Ha! ha! ha! They're ſafe however. What an unaccountable ſet of beings have we got amongſt! This little bar-maid though runs in my head moſt ſtrangely, and drives out the abſurdities of all the

reſt

reſt of the family. She's mine, ſhe muſt be mine, or I'm greatly miſtaken.

Enter HASTINGS.

HASTINGS.

Bleſs me! I quite forgot to tell her that I intended to prepare at the bottom of the garden. Marlow here, and in ſpirits too!

MARLOW.

Give me joy, George! Crown me, ſhadow me with laurels! Well, George, after all, we modeſt fellows don't want for ſucceſs among the women.

HASTINGS.

Some women you mean. But what ſucceſs has your honour's modeſty been crowned with now, that it grows ſo inſolent upon us?

MARLOW.

Didn't you ſee the tempting, briſk, lovely, little thing that runs about the houſe with a bunch of keys to its girdle?

HASTINGS.

Well, and what then?

MARLOW.

She's mine, you rogue you. Such fire, ſuch motion, ſuch eyes, ſuch lips——but, egad! ſhe would not let me kiſs them though.

HASTINGS.

But are you ſo ſure, ſo very ſure of her?

MAR-

MARLOW.

Why, man, ſhe talked of ſhewing me her work above ſtairs, and I am to improve the pattern.

HASTINGS.

But how can you, Charles, go about to rob a woman of her honour?

MARLOW.

Pſhaw! pſhaw! We all know the honour of the bar-maid of an inn. I don't intend to rob her, take my word for it, there's nothing in this houſe, I ſhan't honeſtly pay for.

HASTINGS.

I believe the girl has virtue.

MARLOW.

And if ſhe has, I ſhould be the laſt man in the world that would attempt to corrupt it.

HASTINGS.

You have taken care, I hope, of the caſket I ſent you to lock up? It's in ſafety?

MARLOW.

Yes, yes. It's ſafe enough. I have taken care of it. But how could you think the ſeat of a poſt-coach at an inn-door a place of ſafety? Ah! numbſkull! I have taken better precautions for you than you did for yourſelf.——I have——

HASTINGS.

What!

MARLOW.

I have ſent it to the landlady to keep for you.

HAST-

HASTINGS.

To the landlady!

MARLOW.

The landlady!

HASTINGS.

You did?

MARLOW.

I did. She's to be anſwerable for its forth-coming, you know.

HASTINGS.

Yes, ſhe'll bring it forth, with a witneſs.

MARLOW.

Wasn't I right? I believe you'll allow that I acted prudently upon this occaſion?

HASTINGS.

(*Aſide*) He muſt not ſee my uneaſineſs.

MARLOW.

You ſeem a little diſconcerted though, methinks. Sure nothing has happened?

HASTINGS.

No, nothing. Never was in better ſpirits in all my life. And ſo you left it with the landlady, who, no doubt, very readily undertook the charge?

MARLOW.

Rather too readily. For ſhe not only kept the caſket; but, through her great precaution, was going to keep the meſſenger too. Ha! ha! ha!

HASTINGS.

He! he! he! They're ſafe however.

MAR-

MARLOW.

As a guinea in a miser's purse.

HASTINGS.

(*Aside*) So now all hopes of fortune are at an end, and we must set off without it. (*To him*) Well, Charles, I'll leave you to your meditations on the pretty bar-maid, and, he! he! he! may you be as successful for yourself as you have been for me.

[*Exit.*

MARLOW.

Thank ye, George! I ask no more. Ha! ha! ha!

Enter HARDCASTLE.

HARDCASTLE.

I no longer know my own house. It's turned all topsey-turvey. His servants have got drunk already. I'll bear it no longer, and yet, from my respect for his father, I'll be calm. (*To him*) Mr. Marlow, your servant. I'm your very humble servant.

(*Bowing low.*

MARLOW.

Sir, your humble servant. (*Aside*) What's to be the wonder now?

HARDCASTLE.

I believe, Sir, you must be sensible, Sir, that no man alive ought to be more welcome than your father's son, Sir. I hope you think so?

MAR-

MARLOW.

I do from my ſoul, Sir. I don't want much intreaty. I generally make my father's ſon welcome wherever he goes.

HARDCASTLE.

I believe you do, from my ſoul, Sir. But though I ſay nothing to your own conduct, that of your ſervants is unſufferable. Their manner of drinking is ſetting a very bad example in this houſe, I aſſure you.

MARLOW.

I proteſt, my very good Sir, that is no fault of mine. If they don't drink as they ought they are to blame. I ordered them not to ſpare the cellar. I did, I aſſure you. (*To the ſide ſcene*) Here, let one of my ſervants come up. (*To him*) My poſitive directions were, that as I did not drink myſelf, they ſhould make up for my deficiencies below.

HARDCASTLE.

Then they had your orders for what they do! I'm ſatisfied!

MARLOW.

They had, I aſſure you. You ſhall hear from one of themſelves.

Enter SERVANT, drunk.

MARLOW.

You, Jeremy! Come forward, ſirrah! What were my orders? Were you not told to drink freely, and

and call for what you thought fit, for the good of the houſe?

HARDCASTLE.

(*Aſide*) I begin to loſe my patience.

JEREMY.

Pleaſe your honour, liberty and Fleet-ſtreet for ever! Though I'm but a ſervant, I'm as good as another man. I'll drink for no man before ſupper, Sir, dammy! Good liquor will ſit upon a good ſupper, but a good ſupper will not ſit upon—— hiccup——upon my conſcience, Sir.

MARLOW.

You ſee, my old friend, the fellow is as drunk as he can poſſibly be. I don't know what you'd have more, unleſs you'd have the poor devil ſouſed in a beer-barrel.

HARDCASTLE.

Zounds! he'll drive me diſtracted if I contain myſelf any longer. Mr. Marlow. Sir; I have ſubmitted to your inſolence for more than four hours, and I ſee no likelihood of its coming to an end. I'm now reſolved to be maſter here, Sir, and I deſire that you and your drunken pack may leave my houſe directly.

MARLOW.

Leave your houſe!——Sure you jeſt, my good friend? What, when I'm doing what I can to pleaſe you.

HARD-

HARDCASTLE.

I tell you, Sir, you don't pleafe me; fo I defire you'll leave my houfe.

MARLOW.

Sure you cannot be ferious? at this time o'night, and fuch a night. You only mean to banter me?

HARDCASTLE.

I tell you, Sir, I'm ferious? and, now that my paffions are rouzed, I fay this houfe is mine, Sir; this houfe is mine, and I command you to leave it directly.

MARLOW.

Ha! ha! ha! A puddle in a ftorm. I fhan't ftir a ftep, I affure you. (*In a ferious tone*) This, your houfe, fellow! It's my houfe. This is my houfe. Mine, while I chufe to ftay. What right have you to bid me to leave this houfe, Sir? I never met with fuch impudence, curfe me, never in my whole life before.

HARDCASTLE.

Nor I, confound me if ever I did. To come to my houfe, to call for what he likes, to turn me out of my own chair, to infult the family, to order his fervants to get drunk, and then to tell me "This "houfe is mine, Sir." By all that's impudent it makes me laugh. Ha! ha! ha! Pray, Sir, (*bantering*) as you take the houfe, what think you of taking the reft of the furniture? There's a pair of filver candlefticks, and there's a fire-fcreen, and here's here's a pair of brazen nosed bellows, perhaps you may take a fancy to them?

MARLOW.

Bring me your bill, Sir; bring me your bill, and let's make no more words about it.

HARDCASTLE.

There are a set of prints too. What think you of the rake's progress for your own apartment?

MARLOW.

Bring me your bill, I say; and I'll leave you and your infernal house directly.

HARDCASTLE.

Then there's a mahogany table that you may see your own face in.

MARLOW.

My bill, I say.

HARDCASTLE.

I had forgot the great chair, for your own particular slumbers, after a hearty meal.

MARLOW.

Zounds! bring me my bill, I say, and let's hear no more on't.

HARDCASTLE.

Young man, young man, from your father's letter to me, I was taught to expect a well-bred modest man, as a visitor here, but now I find him no better than a coxcomb and a bully; but he will be down here presently, and shall hear more of it. [*Exit.*

MARLOW.

How's this! Sure I have not miſtaken the houſe! Every thing looks like an inn. The ſervants cry, coming. The attendance is aukward; the bar-maid too to attend us. But ſhe's here, and will further inform me. Whither ſo faſt, child? A word with you.

Enter Miſs HARDCASTLE.

Miſs HARDCASTLE.

Let it be ſhort then. I'm in a hurry. (*Aſide*) I believe he begins to find out his miſtake, but it's too ſoon quite to undeceive him.

MARLOW.

Pray, child, anſwer me one queſtion. What are you, and what may your buſineſs in this houſe be?

Miſs HARDCASTLE.

A relation of the family, Sir.

MARLOW.

What, a poor relation?

Miſs HARDCASTLE.

Yes, Sir. A poor relation appointed to keep the keys, and to ſee that the gueſts want nothing in my power to give them.

MARLOW.

That is, you act as the bar-maid of this inn.

Miſs

Miſs HARDCASTLE.

Inn. O law—What brought that in your head? One of the beſt families in the county keep an inn! Ha! ha! ha! old Mr. Hardcaſtle's houſe an inn!

MARLOW.

Mr. Hardcaſtle's houſe! Is this houſe Mr. Hardcaſtle's houſe, child?

Miſs HARDCASTLE.

Aye, ſure. Whoſe elſe ſhould it be?

MARLOW.

So then all's out, and I have been damnably impoſed on. O, confound my ſtupid head, I ſhall be laugh'd at over the whole town. I ſhall be ſtuck up in caricatura in all the print-ſhops. The *Dulliſſimo Maccaroni*. To miſtake this houſe of all others for an inn, and my father's old friend for an inn-keeper! What a ſwaggering puppy muſt he take me for? What a ſilly puppy do I find myſelf? There again, may I be hanged, my dear, but I miſtook you for the bar-maid.

Miſs HARDCASTLE.

Dear me! dear me! I'm ſure there's nothing in my behaviour to put me upon a level with one of that ſtamp.

MARLOW.

Nothing, my dear, nothing. But I was in for a liſt of blunders, and could not help making you a ſubſcriber. My ſtupidity ſaw every thing the wrong way. I miſtook your aſſiduity for aſſurance, and your ſimplicity for allurement. But its over—This houſe I no more ſhew my face in.

Miſs HARDCASTLE.

I hope, Sir, I have done nothing to diſoblige you. I'm ſure I ſhould be ſorry to affront any gentleman who has been ſo polite, and ſaid ſo many civil things to me. I'm ſure I ſhould be ſorry (*pretending to cry*) if he left the family upon my account. I'm ſure I ſhould be ſorry, people ſaid any thing amiſs, ſince I have no fortune but my character.

MARLOW.

(*Aſide*) By Heaven, ſhe weeps. This is the firſt mark of tenderneſs I ever had from a modeſt woman, and it touches me. (*To her*) Excuſe me, my lovely girl, you are the only part of the family I leave with reluctance. But to be plain with you, the difference of our birth, fortune and education, make an honourable connection impoſſible; and I can never harbour a thought of ſeducing ſimplicity that truſted in my honour, of bringing ruin upon one, whoſe only fault was being too lovely.

Miſs HARDCASTLE.

(*Aſide*) Generous man! I now begin to admire him. (*To him*) But I'm ſure my family is as good as Miſs Hardcaſtle's, and though I'm poor, that's no great misfortune to a contented mind, and, until this moment, I never thought that it was bad to want fortune.

MAR-

MARLOW.

And why now, my pretty ſimplicity?

Miſs HARDCASTLE.

Becauſe it puts me at a diſtance from one, that if I had a thouſand pound I would give it all to.

MARLOW.

(*Aſide*) This ſimplicity bewitches me, ſo that if I ſtay I'm undone. I muſt make one bold effort, and leave her. (*To her*) Your partiality in my favour, my dear, touches me moſt ſenſibly, and were I to live for myſelf alone, I could eaſily fix my choice. But I owe too much to the opinion of the world, too much to the authority of a father, ſo that—I can ſcarcely ſpeak it—it affects me. Farewel. [*Exit.*

Miſs HARDCASTLE.

I never knew half his merit till now. He ſhall not go, if I have power or art to detain him. I'll ſtill preſerve the character in which I *ſtoop'd to conquer*, but will undeceive my papa, who, perhaps, may laugh him out of his reſolution. [*Exit.*

Enter TONY, Miſs NEVILLE.

TONY.

Aye, you may ſteal for yourſelves the next time. I have done my duty. She has got the jewels again, that's a ſure thing; but ſhe believes it was all a miſtake of the ſervants.

Miſs NEVILLE.

But, my dear couſin, ſure you won't forſake us in this diſtreſs. If ſhe in the leaſt ſuſpects that I am going off, I ſhall certainly be locked up, or ſent to my aunt Pedigree's, which is ten times worſe.

TONY.

To be ſure, aunts of all kinds are damn'd bad things. But what can I do? I have got you a pair of horſes that will fly like Whiſtlejacket, and I'm ſure you can't ſay but I have courted you nicely before her face. Here ſhe comes, we muſt court a bit or two more, for fear ſhe ſhould ſuſpect us.

[*They retire, and ſeem to fondle.*

Enter Mrs. HARDCASTLE.

Mrs. HARDCASTLE.

Well, I was greatly fluttered, to be ſure. But my ſon tells me it was all a miſtake of the ſervants. I ſhan't be eaſy, however, till they are fairly married, and then let her keep her own fortune. But what do I ſee! fondling together, as I'm alive. I never ſaw Tony ſo ſprightly before. Ah! have I caught you, my pretty doves! What, billing, exchanging ſtolen glances, and broken murmurs. Ah!

TONY.

As for murmurs, mother, we grumble a little now and then, to be ſure. But there's no love loſt between us.

Mrs.

Mrs. HARDCASTLE.

A mere ſprinkling, Tony, upon the flame, only to make it burn brighter.

Miſs NEVILLE.

Couſin Tony promiſes to give us more of his company at home. Indeed, he ſhan't leave us any more. It won't leave us, couſin Tony, will it?

TONY.

O! it's a pretty creature. No, I'd ſooner leave my horſe in a pound, than leave you when you ſmile upon one ſo. Your laugh makes you ſo becoming.

Miſs NEVILLE.

Agreeable couſin! Who can help admiring that natural humour, that pleaſant, broad, red, thoughtleſs, (*patting his cheek*) ah! it's a bold face.

Mrs. HARDCASTLE.

Pretty innocence!

TONY.

I'm ſure I always lov'd couſin Con's hazle eyes, and her pretty long fingers, that ſhe twiſts this way and that, over the haſpicholls, like a parcel of bobbins.

Mrs. HARDCASTLE.

Ah, he would charm the bird from the tree. I was never ſo happy before. My boy takes after his father, poor Mr. Lumpkin, exactly. The jewels, my dear Con, ſhall be yours incontinently. You ſhall have them. Isn't he a ſweet boy, my dear?

You ſhall be married to-morrow, and we'll put off the reſt of his education, like Dr. Drowſy's ſermons, to a fitter opportunity,

Enter DIGGORY.

DIGGORY.

Where's the 'ſquire? I have got a letter for your worſhip.

TONY.

Give it to my mamma. She reads all my letters firſt.

DIGGORY.

I had orders to deliver it into your own hands,

TONY.

Who does it come from?

DIGGORY.

Your worſhip mun aſk that o' the letter itſelf.

TONY.

I could wiſh to know, though (*turning the letter, and gazing on it.*)

Miſs NEVILLE.

(*Aſide*) Undone! undone! A letter to him from Haſtings. I know the hand. If my aunt ſees it we are ruined for ever. I'll keep her employ'd a little if I can. (*To Mrs. Hardcaſtle*) But I have not told you, madam, of my couſin's ſmart anſwer juſt now to Mr. Marlow. We ſo laugh'd—You muſt know, madam,—This way a little, for he muſt not hear us, [*They confer.*

TONY.

TONY.

(*Still gazing*) A damn'd cramp piece of penmanſhip, as ever I ſaw in my life. I can read your print hand very well. But here there are ſuch handles, and ſhanks, and daſhes, that one can ſcarce tell the head from the tail. "To Anthony Lump-"kin, eſquire." It's very odd, I can read the outſide of my letters, where my own name is, well enough. But when I come to open it, it's all—— buzz. That's hard, very hard; for the inſide of the letter is always the cream of the correſpondence.

Mrs. HARDCASTLE.

Ha! ha! ha! Very well, very well. And ſo my ſon was too hard for the philoſopher.

Miſs NEVILLE.

Yes, madam; but you muſt hear the reſt, madam. A little more this way, or he may hear us. You'll hear how he puzzled him again.

Mrs. HARDCASTLE.

He ſeems ſtrangely puzzled now himſelf, methinks.

TONY.

(*Still gazing*) A damn'd up and down hand, as if it was diſguiſed in liquor. (*Reading*) Dear Sir. Aye, that's that. Then there's an M, and a T, and an S, but whether the next be an izzard or an R, confound me, I cannot tell.

Mrs.

Mrs. HARDCASTLE.

What's that, my dear. Can I give you any affiftance?

Mifs NEVILLE.

Pray, aunt, let me read it. No body reads a cramp hand better than I. (*twitching the letter from her*) Do you know who it is from?

TONY.

Can't tell, except from Dick Ginger the feeder.

Mifs NEVILLE.

Aye, fo it is, (*pretending to read*) Dear 'fquire, hoping that you're in health, as I am at this prefent. The gentlemen of the Shake-bag club has cut the gentlemen of Goofe-green quite out of feather. The odds——um—odd battle——um—long fighting—um—here, here, it's all about cocks and fighting; it's of no confequence, here, put it up, put it up. [*Thrufting the crumpled letter upon him.*

TONY.

But I tell you, mifs, it's of all the confequence in the world. I would not lofe the reft of it for a guinea. Here, mother, do you make it out. Of no confequence! [*Giving* Mrs. Hardcaftle *the letter.*

Mrs. HARDCASTLE.

How's this! (*reads*) "Dear 'fquire, I'm now "waiting for Mifs Neville, with a poft-chaife and "pair, at the bottom of the garden, but I find my "horfes yet unable to perform the journey. I ex-"pect you'll affift us with a pair of frefh horfes, as

"you

" you promiſed. Diſpatch is neceſſary, as the hag " (aye the hag) your mother, will otherwiſe ſuſpect " us. Yours, Haſtings." Grant me patience. I ſhall run diſtracted. My rage choaks me.

Miſs NEVILLE.

I hope, madam, you'll ſuſpend your reſentment for a few moments, and not impute to me any impertinence, or ſiniſter deſign, that belongs to another.

Mrs. HARDCASTLE.

(*Curteſying very low.*) Fine ſpoken, madam, you are moſt miraculouſly polite and engaging, and quite the very pink of curteſy and circumſpection, madam. (*Changing her tone*) And you, you great ill-faſhioned oaf, with ſcarce ſenſe enough to keep your mouth ſhut. Were you too join'd againſt me? But I'll defeat all your plots in a moment. As for you, madam, ſince you have got a pair of freſh horſes ready, it would be cruel to diſappoint them. So, if you pleaſe, inſtead of running away with your ſpark, prepare, this very moment, to run off with me. Your old aunt Pedigree will keep you ſecure, I'll warrant me. You too, Sir, may mount your horſe, and guard us upon the way. Here, Thomas, Roger, Diggory, I'll ſhew you, that I wiſh you better than you do yourſelves. [*Exit.*

Miſs NEVILLE.

So now I'm completely ruined.

TONY.

Aye, that's a ſure thing.

Miſs

Miſs NEVILLE.

What better could be expected from being connected with ſuch a ſtupid fool, and after all the nods and ſigns I made him?

TONY.

By the laws, Miſs, it was your own cleverneſs, and not my ſtupidity, that did your buſineſs. You were ſo nice and ſo buſy with your Shake-bags and Gooſe-greens, that I thought you could never be making believe.

Enter HASTINGS.

HASTINGS.

So, Sir, I find by my ſervant, that you have ſhewn my letter, and betray'd us. Was this well done, young gentleman?

TONY.

Here's another. Aſk Miſs there who betray'd you? Ecod, it was her doing, not mine.

Enter MARLOW.

MARLOW.

So I have been finely uſed here among you. Rendered contemptible, driven into ill manners, deſpiſed, inſulted, laughed at.

TONY.

Here's another. We ſhall have old Bedlam broke looſe preſently.

Miſs

Miſs NEVILLE.

And there, Sir, is the gentleman to whom we all owe every obligation.

MARLOW.

What can I ſay to him, a mere boy, an idiot, whoſe ignorance and age are a protection.

HASTINGS.

A poor contemptible booby, that would but diſgrace correction.

Miſs NEVILLE.

Yet with cunning and malice enough to make himſelf merry with all our embarraſſments.

HASTINGS.

An inſenſible cub.

MARLOW.

Replete with tricks and miſchief.

TONY.

Baw! damme, but I'll fight you both one after the other,——with baſkets.

MARLOW.

As for him, he's below reſentment. But your conduct, Mr. Haſtings, requires an explanation. You knew of my miſtakes, yet would not undeceive me.

HASTINGS.

Tortured as I am with my own diſappointments, is this a time for explanations. It is not friendly, Mr. Marlow.

MARLOW.

But, Sir—

Miſs

Miſs Neville.

Mr. Marlow, we never kept on your miſtake, till it was too late to undeceive you. Be pacified.

Enter Servant.

Servant.

My miſtreſs deſires you'll get ready immediately, madam. The horſes are putting to. Your hat and things are in the next room. We are to go thirty miles before morning. [*Exit ſervant.*

Miſs Neville.

Well, well; I'll come preſently.

Marlow.

(*To Haſtings*) Was it well done, Sir, to aſſiſt in rendering me ridiculous. To hang me out for the ſcorn of all my acquaintance. Depend upon it, Sir, I ſhall expect an explanation.

Hastings.

Was it well done, Sir, if you're upon that ſubject, to deliver what I entruſted to yourſelf, to the care of another, Sir.

Miſs Neville.

Mr. Haſtings. Mr. Marlow. Why will you increaſe my diſtreſs by this groundleſs diſpute? I implore, I intreat you——

Enter

Enter SERVANT.

SERVANT.

Your cloak, madam. My miſtreſs is impatient.

[*Exit* Servant.

Miſs NEVILLE.

I come. Pray be pacified. If I leave you thus, I ſhall die with apprehenſion.

Enter SERVANT.

SERVANT.

Your fan, muff, and gloves, madam. The horſes are waiting.

Miſs NEVILLE.

O, Mr. Marlow! if you knew what a ſcene of conſtraint and ill-nature lies before me, I'm ſure it would convert your reſentment into pity.

MARLOW.

I'm ſo diſtracted with a variety of paſſions, that I don't know what I do. Forgive me, madam. George, forgive me. You know my haſty temper, and ſhould not exaſperate it.

HASTINGS.

The torture of my ſituation is my only excuſe.

Miſs NEVILLE.

Well, my dear Haſtings, if you have that eſteem for me that I think, that I am ſure you have, your conſtancy for three years will but encreaſe the happineſs of our future connexion. If—

Mrs.

Mrs. Hardcastle.

(*Within*) Miſs Neville. Conſtance, why Conſtance, I ſay.

Miſs Neville.

I'm coming. Well, conſtancy. Remember, conſtancy is the word. [*Exit.*

Hastings.

My heart! how can I ſupport this. To be ſo near happineſs, and ſuch happineſs!

Marlow.

(*To Tony*) You ſee now, young gentleman, the effects of your folly. What might be amuſement to you, is here diſappointment, and even diſtreſs.

Tony.

(*From a reverie*) Ecod, I have hit it. It's here. Your hands. Yours and yours, my poor Sulky. My boots there, ho. Meet me two hours hence at the bottom of the garden; and if you don't find Tony Lumpkin a more good-natur'd fellow than you thought for, I'll give you leave to take my beſt horſe, and Bet Bouncer into the bargain. Come along. My boots, ho! [*Exeunt.*

ACT THE FIFTH.

SCENE continues.

Enter HASTINGS and SERVANT.

HASTINGS.

YOU ſaw the old lady and Miſs Neville drive off, you ſay.

SERVANT.

Yes, your honour. They went off in a poſt coach, and the young 'ſquire went on horſeback. They're thirty miles off by this time.

HASTINGS.

Then all my hopes are over.

SERVANT.

Yes, Sir. Old Sir Charles is arrived. He and the old gentleman of the houſe have been laughing at Mr. Marlow's miſtake this half hour. They are coming this way.

HASTINGS.

Then I muſt not be ſeen. So now to my fruitleſs appointment at the bottom of the garden. This is about the time. [*Exit.*

Enter Sir CHARLES and HARDCASTLE.

HARDCASTLE.

Ha! ha! ha! The peremptory tone in which he ſent forth his ſublime commands.

Sir CHARLES.

And the reſerve with which I ſuppoſe he treated all your advances.

HARDCASTLE.

And yet he might have ſeen ſomething in me above a common inn-keeper, too.

Sir CHARLES.

Yes, Dick, but he miſtook you for an uncommon inn-keeper, ha! ha! ha!

HARDCASTLE.

Well, I'm in too good ſpirits to think of any thing but joy. Yes, my dear friend, this union of our families will make our perſonal friendſhips hereditary; and though my daughter's fortune is but ſmall——

Sir CHARLES.

Why, Dick, will you talk of fortune to me? My ſon is poſſeſſed of more than a competence already, and can want nothing but a good and virtuous girl to ſhare his happineſs and encreaſe it. If they like each other, as you ſay they do——

HARDCASTLE.

If, man! I tell you they do like each other. My daughter as good as told me ſo.

Sir

Sir CHARLES.

But girls are apt to flatter themſelves, you know.

HARDCASTLE.

I ſaw him graſp her hand in the warmeſt manner myſelf; and here he comes to put you out of your ifs, I warrant him.

Enter MARLOW.

MARLOW.

I come, Sir, once more, to aſk pardon for my ſtrange conduct. I can ſcarce reflect on my inſolence without confuſion.

HARDCASTLE.

Tut, boy, a trifle. You take it too gravely. An hour or two's laughing with my daughter will ſet all to rights again. She'll never like you the worſe for it.

MARLOW.

Sir, I ſhall be always proud of her approbation.

HARDCASTLE.

Approbation is but a cold word, Mr. Marlow; if I am not deceived, you have ſomething more than approbation thereabouts. You take me.

MARLOW.

Really, Sir, I have not that happineſs.

HARDCASTLE.

Come, boy, I'm an old fellow, and know what's what, as well as you that are younger. I know what has paſt between you ; but mum.

MARLOW.

Sure, Sir, nothing has paſt between us but the moſt profound reſpect on my ſide, and the moſt diſtant reſerve on hers. You don't think, Sir, that my impudence has been paſt upon all the reſt of the family.

HARDCASTLE.

Impudence! No, I don't ſay that—not quite impudence—though girls like to be play'd with, and rumpled a little too ſometimes. But ſhe has told no tales, I aſſure you.

MARLOW.

I never gave her the ſlighteſt cauſe.

HARDCASTLE.

Well, well, I like modeſty in its place well enough. But this is over-acting, young gentleman. You may be open. Your father and I will like you the better for it.

MARLOW.

May I die, Sir, if I ever——

HARDCASTLE.

I tell you, ſhe don't diſlike you ; and as I'm ſure you like her——

MARLOW.

Dear, Sir—I proteſt, Sir——

HARD-

HARDCASTLE.

I ſee no reaſon why you ſhould not be joined as faſt as the parſon can tie you.

MARLOW.

But hear me, Sir——

HARDCASTLE.

Your father approves the match, I admire it, every moment's delay will be doing miſchief, ſo—

MARLOW.

But why won't you hear me? By all that's juſt and true, I never gave Miſs Hardcaſtle the ſlighteſt mark of my attachment, or even the moſt diſtant hint to ſuſpect me of affection. We had but one interview, and that was formal, modeſt and unintereſting.

HARDCASTLE.

(*Aſide*) This fellow's formal modeſt impudence is beyond bearing.

Sir CHARLES.

And you never graſp'd her hand, or made any proteſtations.

MARLOW.

As Heaven is my witneſs, I came down in obedience to your commands. I ſaw the lady without emotion, and parted without reluctance. I hope you'll exact no further proofs of my duty, nor prevent me from leaving a houſe in which I ſuffer ſo many mortifications. [*Exit.*

Sir CHARLES.

I'm aſtoniſhed at the air of ſincerity with which he parted.

HARDCASTLE.

And I'm aſtoniſh'd at the deliberate intrepidity of his aſſurance.

Sir CHARLES.

I dare pledge my life and honour upon his truth.

HARDCASTLE.

Here comes my daughter, and I would ſtake my happineſs upon her veracity.

Enter Miſs HARDCASTLE.

HARDCASTLE.

Kate, come hither, child. Anſwer us ſincerely, and without reſerve; has Mr. Marlow made you any profeſſions of love and affection?

Miſs HARDCASTLE.

The queſtion is very abrupt, Sir! But ſince you require unreſerved ſincerity, I think he has.

HARDCASTLE.

(*To Sir Charles*) You ſee.

Sir CHARLES.

And pray, madam, have you and my ſon had more than one interview?

Miſs HARDCASTLE.

Yes, Sir, ſeveral.

HARD-

HARDCASTLE.

(*To Sir Charles*) You ſee.

Sir CHARLES.

But did he profeſs any attachment?

Miſs HARDCASTLE.

A laſting one.

Sir CHARLES.

Did he talk of love?

Miſs HARDCASTLE.

Much, Sir.

Sir CHARLES.

Amazing! And all this formally?

Miſs HARDCASTLE.

Formally.

HARDCASTLE.

Now, my friend, I hope you are ſatisfied.

Sir CHARLES.

And how did he behave, madam?

Miſs HARDCASTLE.

As moſt profeſt admirers do. Said ſome civil things of my face, talked much of his want of merit, and the greatneſs of mine; mentioned his heart, gave a ſhort tragedy ſpeech, and ended with pretended rapture.

Sir CHARLES.

Now I'm perfectly convinced, indeed. I know his converſation among women to be modeſt and ſubmiſſive. This forward canting ranting manner by no means deſcribes him, and, I am confident, he never ſate for the picture.

Miſs HARDCASTLE.

Then what, Sir, if I ſhould convince you to your face of my ſincerity? If you and my papa, in about half an hour, will place yourſelves behind that ſcreen, you ſhall hear him declare his paſſion to me in perſon.

Sir CHARLES.

Agreed. And if I find him what you deſcribe, all my happineſs in him muſt have an end. [*Exit.*

Miſs HARDCASTLE.

And if you don't find him what I deſcribe——I fear my happineſs muſt never have a beginning.

[*Exeunt.*

SCENE changes to the Back of the Garden.

Enter HASTINGS,

HASTINGS.

What an idiot am I, to wait here for a fellow, who probably takes a delight in mortifying me. He never intended to be punctual, and I'll wait no longer. What do I ſee! It is he! and perhaps with news of my Conſtance.

Enter TONY, booted and ſpattered.

HASTINGS.

My honeſt 'ſquire! I now find you a man of your word. This looks like friendſhip.

TONY,

TONY.

Aye, I'm your friend, and the beſt friend you have in the world, if you knew but all. This riding by night, by the bye, is curſedly tireſome. It has ſhook me worſe than the baſket of a ſtage-coach.

HASTINGS.

But how? where did you leave your fellow travellers? Are they in ſafety? Are they houſed?

TONY.

Five and twenty miles in two hours and a half is no ſuch bad driving. The poor beaſts have ſmoaked for it: rabbet me, but I'd rather ride forty miles after a fox, than ten with ſuch varment.

HASTINGS.

Well, but where have you left the ladies? I die with impatience.

TONY.

Left them! Why where ſhould I leave them, but where I found them?

HASTINGS.

This is a riddle.

TONY.

Riddle me this then. What's that goes round the houſe, and round the houſe, and never touches the houſe?

HASTINGS.

I'm ſtill aſtray.

TONY.

TONY.

Why that's it, mon. I have led them aſtray. By jingo, there's not a pond or ſlough within five miles of the place but they can tell the taſte of.

HASTINGS.

Ha! ha! ha! I underſtand; you took them in a round, while they ſuppoſed themſelves going forward, and ſo you have at laſt brought them home again.

TONY.

You ſhall hear. I firſt took them down Feather-bed-lane, where we ſtuck faſt in the mud. I then rattled them crack over the ſtones of Up-and-down Hill—I then introduced them to the gibbet on Heavy-tree Heath, and from that with a circumbendibus, I fairly lodged them in the horſe-pond at the bottom of the garden.

HASTINGS.

But no accident, I hope.

TONY.

No, no. Only mother is confoundedly frightened. She thinks herſelf forty-miles off. She's ſick of the journey, and the cattle can ſcarce crawl. So if your own horſes be ready, you may whip off with couſin, and I'll be bound that no ſoul here can budge a foot to follow you.

HASTINGS.

My dear friend, how can I be grateful?

TONY.

TONY.

Aye, now its dear friend, noble 'ſquire. Juſt now, it was all idiot, cub, and run me through the guts. Damn your way of fighting, I ſay. After we take a knock in this part of the country, we kiſs and be friends. But if you had run me through the guts, then I ſhould be dead, and you might go kiſs the hangman.

HASTINGS.

The rebuke is juſt. But I muſt haſten to relieve Miſs Neville; if you keep the old lady employed, I promiſe to take care of the young one.

[*Exit* Haſtings.

TONY.

Never fear me. Here ſhe comes. Vaniſh. She's got from the pond, and draggled up to the waiſt like a mermaid.

Enter Mrs. HARDCASTLE.

Mrs. HARDCASTLE.

Oh, Tony, I'm killed. Shook. Battered to death. I ſhall never ſurvive it. That laſt jolt that laid us againſt the quickſet hedge has done my buſineſs.

TONY.

Alack, mamma, it was all your own fault. You would be for running away by night, without knowing one inch of the way.

Mrs.

Mrs. HARDCASTLE.

I wiſh we were at home again. I never met ſo many accidents in ſo ſhort a journey. Drench'd in the mud, overturned in a ditch, ſtuck faſt in a ſlough, jolted to a jelly, and at laſt to loſe our way. Whereabouts do you think we are, Tony?

TONY.

By my gueſs we ſhould come upon Crackſkull common, about forty miles from home.

Mrs. HARDCASTLE.

O lud! O lud! The moſt notorious ſpot in all the country. We only want a robbery to make a complete night on't.

TONY.

Don't be afraid, mamma, don't be afraid. Two of the five that kept here are hanged, and the other three may not find us. Don't be afraid. Is that a man that's galloping behind us? No; it's only a tree. Don't be afraid.

Mrs. HARDCASTLE.

The fright will certainly kill me.

TONY.

Do you ſee any thing like a black hat moving behind the thicket?

Mrs. HARDCASTLE.

O death!

TONY.

No, it's only a cow. Don't be afraid, mamma; don't be afraid.

Mrs. HARDCASTLE.

As I'm alive, Tony, I ſee a man coming towards us. Ah! I'm ſure on't. If he perceives us we are undone.

TONY.

(*Aſide*) Father-in-law, by all that's unlucky, come to take one of his night walks. (*To her*) Ah, it's a highwayman, with piſtols as long as my arm. A damn'd ill-looking fellow.

Mrs. HARDCASTLE.

Good Heaven defend us! He approaches.

TONY.

Do you hide yourſelf in that thicket, and leave me to manage him. If there be any danger I'll cough and cry hem. When I cough be ſure to keep cloſe. [*Mrs.* Hardcaſtle *hides behind a tree in the back ſcene.*

Enter HARDCASTLE.

HARDCASTLE.

I'm miſtaken, or I heard voices of people in want of help. Oh, Tony, is that you? I did not expect you ſo ſoon back. Are your mother and her charge in ſafety?

TONY.

Very ſafe, Sir, at my aunt Pedigree's. Hem.

Mrs. HARDCASTLE.

(*From behind*) Ah death! I find there's danger.

HARD-

HARDCASTLE.

Forty miles in three hours; ſure, that's too much, my youngſter.

TONY.

Stout horſes and willing minds make ſhort journeys, as they ſay. Hem.

Mrs. HARDCASTLE.

(*From behind*) Sure he'll do the dear boy no harm.

HARDCASTLE.

But I heard a voice here; I ſhould be glad to know from whence it came.

TONY.

It was I, Sir, talking to myſelf, Sir. I was ſaying that forty miles in four hours was very good going. Hem. As to be ſure it was. Hem. I have got a ſort of cold by being out in the air. We'll go in, if you pleaſe. Hem.

HARDCASTLE.

But if you talk'd to yourſelf, you did not anſwer yourſelf. I am certain I heard two voices, and am reſolved (*raiſing his voice*) to find the other out.

Mrs. HARDCASTLE.

(*From behind*) Oh! he's coming to find me out. Oh!

TONY.

What need you go, Sir, if I tell you. Hem. I'll lay down my life for the truth—hem—I'll tell you all, Sir. [*Detaining him.*

HARD-

HARDCASTLE.

I tell you, I will not be detained. I inſiſt on ſeeing. It's in vain to expect I'll believe you.

Mrs. HARDCASTLE.

(*Running forward from behind*) O lud! he'll murder my poor boy, my darling. Here good gentleman, whet your rage upon me. Take my money, my life, but ſpare that young gentleman, ſpare my child, if you have any mercy.

HARDCASTLE.

My wife! as I'm a Chriſtian. From whence can ſhe come? or what does ſhe mean?

Mrs. HARDCASTLE.

(*Kneeling*) Take compaſſion on us, good Mr. Highwayman. Take our money, our watches, all we have, but ſpare our lives. We will never bring you to juſtice, indeed we won't, good Mr. Highwayman.

HARDCASTLE.

I believe the woman's out of her ſenſes. What, Dorothy, don't you know me?

Mrs. HARDCASTLE.

Mr. Hardcaſtle, as I'm alive! My fears blinded me. But who, my dear, could have expected to meet you here, in this frightful place, ſo far from home? What has brought you to follow us?

HARDCASTLE.

Sure, Dorothy, you have not loſt your wits? So far from home, when you are within forty yards of

your

your own door. (*To him*) This is one of your old tricks, you gracelefs rogue you. (*To her*) Don't you know the gate, and the mulberry-tree; and don't you remember the horfepond, my dear?

Mrs. HARDCASTLE.

Yes, I fhall remember the horfepond as long as I live; I have caught my death in it. (*To* Tony) And is it to you, you gracelefs varlet, I owe all this. I'll teach you to abufe your mother, I will.

TONY.

Ecod, mother, all the parifh fays you have fpoil'd me, and fo you may take the fruits on't.

Mrs. HARDCASTLE.

I'll fpoil you, I will.

[*Follows him off the Stage. Exit.*

HARDCASTLE.

There's morality, however, in his reply. [*Exit.*

Enter HASTINGS and Mifs NEVILLE.

HASTINGS.

My dear Conftance, why will you deliberate thus? If we delay a moment, all is loft for ever. Pluck up a little refolution, and we fhall foon be out of the reach of her malignity.

Mifs NEVILLE.

I find it impoffible. My fpirits are fo funk with the agitations I have fuffered, that I am unable to face any new danger. Two or three years patience will at laft crown us with happinefs.

HAST-

HASTINGS.

Such a tedious delay is worſe than inconſtancy. Let us fly, my charmer. Let us date our happineſs from this very moment. Periſh fortune! Love and content will encreaſe what we poſſeſs beyond a monarch's revenue. Let me prevail?

Miſs NEVILLE.

No, Mr. Haſtings; no. Prudence once more comes to my relief, and I will obey its dictates. In the moment of paſſion, fortune may be deſpiſed, but it ever produces a laſting repentance. I'm reſolved to apply to Mr. Hardcaſtle's compaſſion and juſtice for redreſs.

HASTINGS.

But though he had the will, he has not the power to relieve you.

Miſs NEVILLE.

But he has influence, and upon that I am reſolved to rely.

HASTINGS.

I have no hopes. But ſince you perſiſt, I muſt reluctantly obey you. [*Exeunt.*

SCENE changes.

Enter Sir CHARLES and Miſs HARDCASTLE.

Sir CHARLES.

What a ſituation am I in! If what you ſay appears, I ſhall then find a guilty ſon. If what he ſays be true, I ſhall then loſe one, that, of all others, I moſt wiſh'd for a daughter.

Miſs HARDCASTLE.

I am proud of your approbation, and to ſhew I merit it, if you place yourſelves as I directed, you ſhall hear his explicit declaration. But he comes.

Sir CHARLES.

I'll to your father, and keep him to the appointment. [*Exit Sir* Charles.

Enter MARLOW.

MARLOW.

Though prepar'd for ſetting out, I come once more to take leave, nor did I, till this moment, know the pain I feel in the ſeparation.

Miſs HARDCASTLE.

(*In her own natural manner*) I believe theſe ſufferings cannot be very great, Sir, which you can ſo eaſily remove. A day or two longer, perhaps, might leſſen your uneaſineſs, by ſhewing the little value of what you now think proper to regret.

MARLOW.

(*Aſide*) This girl every moment improves upon me. (*To her*) It muſt not be, madam. I have already trifled too long with my heart. My very pride begins to ſubmit to my paſſion. The diſparity of education and fortune, the anger of a parent, and the contempt of my equals, begin to loſe their weight;

weight; and nothing can restore me to myself, but this painful effort of resolution.

Miss HARDCASTLE.

Then go, Sir. I'll urge nothing more to detain you. Though my family be as good as hers you came down to visit, and my education, I hope, not inferior, what are these advantages without equal affluence? I must remain contented with the slight approbation of imputed merit; I must have only the mockery of your addresses, while all your serious aims are fixed on fortune.

Enter HARDCASTLE and Sir CHARLES from behind.

Sir CHARLES.

Here, behind this screen.

HARDCASTLE.

Aye, aye, make no noise. I'll engage my Kate covers him with confusion at last.

MARLOW.

By Heavens, madam, fortune was ever my smallest consideration. Your beauty at first caught my eye; for who could see that without emotion. But every moment that I converse with you, steals in some new grace, heightens the picture, and gives it stronger expression. What at first seem'd rustic plainness, now appears refin'd simplicity. What ſeem'd forward aſſurance, now ſtrikes me as the reſult of courageous innocence, and conſcious virtue.

Sir CHARLES.

What can it mean? He amazes me!

HARDCASTLE.

I told you how it would be. Huſh!

MARLOW.

I am now determined to ſtay, madam, and I have too good an opinion of my father's diſcernment, when he ſees you, to doubt his approbation.

Miſs HARDCASTLE.

No, Mr. Marlow, I will not, cannot detain you. Do you think I could ſuffer a connexion, in which there is the ſmalleſt room for repentance? Do you think I would take the mean advantage of a tranſient paſſion, to load you with confuſion? Do you think I could ever reliſh that happineſs, which was acquired by leſſening yours?

MARLOW.

By all that's good, I can have no happineſs but what's in your power to grant me. Nor ſhall I ever feel repentance, but in not having ſeen your merits before. I will ſtay, even contrary to your wiſhes; and though you ſhould perſiſt to ſhun me, I will make my reſpectful aſſiduities atone for the levity of my paſt conduct.

Miſs HARDCASTLE.

Sir, I muſt entreat you'll deſiſt. As our acquaintance began, ſo let it end, in indifference. I might

might have given an hour or two to levity; but seriously, Mr. Marlow, do you think I could ever submit to a connexion, where I must appear mercenary, and you imprudent? do you think I could ever catch at the confident addresses of a secure admirer?

MARLOW.

(*Kneeling*) Does this look like security? Does this look like confidence? No, madam, every moment that shews me your merit, only serves to encrease my diffidence and confusion. Here let me continue——

Sir CHARLES.

I can hold it no longer. Charles, Charles, how hast thou deceived me! Is this your indifference, your uninteresting conversation!

HARDCASTLE.

Your cold contempt; your formal interview. What have you to say now?

MARLOW.

That I'm all amazement! What can it mean!

HARDCASTLE.

It means that you can say and unsay things at pleasure. That you can address a lady in private, and deny it in public; that you have one story for us, and another for my daughter!

MARLOW.

Daughter!—this lady your daughter!

HARDCASTLE.

Yes, Sir, my only daughter. My Kate, whoſe elſe ſhould ſhe be?

MARLOW.

Oh, the devil!

Miſs HARDCASTLE.

Yes, Sir, that very identical tall ſquinting lady you were pleaſed to take me for, (*curteſying*) ſhe that you addreſſed as the mild, modeſt, ſentimental man of gravity, and the bold forward agreeable Rattle of the ladies club; ha! ha! ha!

MARLOW.

Zounds, there's no bearing this; it's worſe than death.

Miſs HARDCASTLE.

In which of your characters, Sir, will you give us leave to addreſs you. As the faultering gentleman, with looks on the ground, that ſpeaks juſt to be heard, and hates hypocriſy; or the loud confident creature, that keeps it up with Mrs. Mantrap, and old Miſs Biddy Buckſkin, till three in the morning; ha! ha! ha!

MARLOW.

O, curſe on my noiſy head. I never attempted to be impudent yet, that I was not taken down. I muſt be gone.

HARD-

HARDCASTLE.

By the hand of my body, but you ſhall not. I ſee it was all a miſtake, and I am rejoiced to find it. You ſhall not, Sir, I tell you. I know ſhe'll forgive you. Won't you forgive him, Kate. We'll all forgive you. Take courage, man.

[*They retire, ſhe tormenting him to the back ſcene.*

Enter Mrs. HARDCASTLE, TONY.

Mrs. HARDCASTLE.

So, ſo, they're gone off. Let them go, I care not.

HARDCASTLE.

Who gone?

Mrs. HARDCASTLE.

My dutiful niece and her gentleman, Mr. Haſtings, from town. He who came down with our modeſt viſitor here.

Sir CHARLES.

Who, my honeſt George Haſtings! As worthy a fellow as lives, and the girl could not have made a more prudent choice.

HARDCASTLE.

Then, by the hand of my body, I'm proud of the connexion.

Mrs. HARDCASTLE.

Well, if he has taken away the lady, he has not taken her fortune, that remains in this family to confole us for her lofs.

HARDCASTLE.

Sure, Dorothy, you would not be fo mercenary?

Mrs. HARDCASTLE.

Aye, that's my affair, not yours. But you know if your fon, when of age, refufes to marry his coufin, her whole fortune is then at her own difpofal.

HARDCASTLE.

Aye, but he's not of age, and fhe has not thought proper to wait for his refufal.

Enter HASTINGS and Mifs NEVILLE.

Mrs. HARDCASTLE.

(*Afide*) What, returned fo foon! I begin not to like it.

HASTINGS.

(*To Hardcaftle*) For my late attempt to fly off with your niece, let my prefent confufion be my punifhment. We are now come back, to appeal from your juftice to your humanity. By her father's confent, I firft paid her my addreffes, and our paffions were firft founded in duty.

Miſs NEVILLE.

Since his death, I have been obliged to ſtoop to diſſimulation to avoid oppreſſion. In an hour of levity, I was ready even to give up my fortune to ſecure my choice. But I'm now recover'd from the deluſion, and hope from your tenderneſs what is denied me from a nearer connexion.

Mrs. HARDCASTLE.

Pſhaw, pſhaw, this is all but the whining end of a modern novel.

HARDCASTLE.

Be it what it will, I'm glad they're come back to reclaim their due. Come hither, Tony boy. Do you refuſe this lady's hand whom I now offer you?

TONY.

What ſignifies my refuſing. You know I can't refuſe her till I'm of age, father.

HARDCASTLE.

While I thought concealing your age, boy, was likely to conduce to your improvement, I concurred with your mother's deſire to keep it ſecret. But ſince I find ſhe turns it to a wrong uſe, I muſt now declare, you have been of age theſe three months.

TONY.

Of age! Am I of age, father?

HARDCASTLE.

Above three months.

TONY.

Then you'll ſee the firſt uſe I'll make of my liberty. (*Taking Miſs* Neville'*s hand*) Witneſs all men by theſe preſents, that I, Anthony Lumpkin, eſquire, of BLANK place, refuſe you, Conſtantia Neville, ſpinſter, of no place at all, for my true and lawful wife. So Conſtance Neville may marry whom ſhe pleaſes, and Tony Lumpkin is his own man again.

Sir CHARLES.

O brave 'ſquire!

HASTINGS.

My worthy friend!

Mrs. HARDCASTLE.

My undutiful offspring!

MARLOW.

Joy, my dear George, I give you joy ſincerely. And could I prevail upon my little tyrant here to be leſs arbitrary, I ſhould be the happieſt man alive, if you would return me the favour.

HASTINGS.

(*To Miſs* Hardcaſtle) Come, madam, you are now driven to the very laſt ſcene of all your contrivances. I know you like him, I'm ſure he loves you, and you muſt and ſhall have him.

HARD-

HARDCASTLE.

(*Joining their hands*) And I ſay ſo too. And, Mr. Marlow, if ſhe makes as good a wife as ſhe has a daughter, I don't believe you'll ever repent your bargain. So now to ſupper. To-morrow we ſhall gather all the poor of the pariſh about us, and the miſtakes of the night ſhall be crowned with a merry morning; ſo, boy, take her; and as you have been miſtaken in the miſtreſs, my wiſh is, that you may never be miſtaken in the wife.

EPILOGUE.

BY DR GOLDSMITH.

WELL, having ſtoop'd to conquer with ſucceſs,
And gain'd a huſband without aid from dreſs,
Still as a bar-maid, I could wiſh it too,
As I have conquer'd him to conquer you:
And let me ſay, for all your reſolution,
That pretty bar-maids have done execution.
Our life is all a play, compos'd to pleaſe,
"We have our exits and our entrances."
The firſt act ſhews the ſimple country maid,
Harmleſs and young, of every thing afraid;
Bluſhes when hir'd, and with unmeaning action,
"I hopes as how to give you ſatisfaction."
Her ſecond act diſplays a livelier ſcene.—
Th' unbluſhing bar-maid of a country inn,
Who whiſks about the houſe, at market caters,
Talks loud, coquets the gueſts, and ſcolds the waiters.
Next the ſcene ſhifts to town, and there ſhe ſoars,
The chop-houſe toaſt of ogling *connoiſſeurs.*
On 'ſquires and cits ſhe there diſplays her arts,
And on the gridiron broils her lover's hearts—

And as ſhe ſmiles, her triumphs to compleat,
Even common councilmen forget to eat.
The fourth act ſhews her wedded to the 'ſquire,
And madam now begins to hold it higher;
Pretends to taſte, at operas cries caro,
And quits her Nancy Dawſon, for Che Faro.
Doats upon dancing, and in all her pride,
Swims round the room, the Heinell of Cheapſide:
Ogles and leers with artificial ſkill,
Till having loſt in age the power to kill,
She ſits all night at cards, and ogles at ſpadille.
Such, through our lives, the eventful hiſtory—
The fifth and laſt act ſtill remains for me.
The bar-maid now for your protection prays,
Turns female Barriſter, and pleads for Bays.

EPILOGUE,

TO BE SPOKEN IN THE CHARACTER OF

TONY LUMPKIN.*

BY J. CRADDOCK, ESQ.

WELL—now all's ended—and my comrades gone,
Pray what becomes of mother's nonly ſon?
A hopeful blade!—in town I'll fix my ſtation,
And try to make a bluſter in the nation.
As for my couſin Neville, I renounce her,
Off—in a crack—I'll carry big Bett Bouncer.

Why ſhould not I in the great world appear?
I ſoon ſhall have a thouſand pounds a year?
No matter what a man may here inherit,
In London—'gad, they have ſome regard to ſpirit.
I ſee the horſes prancing up the ſtreets,
And big Bett Bouncer, bobs to all ſhe meets;
Then hoikes to jiggs and paſtimes ev'ry night—
Not to the plays—they ſay it a'n't polite;

* This came too late to be ſpoken.

To

To Sadler's-Wells perhaps, or operas go,
And once by chance, to the roratorio.
Thus here and there, for ever up and down,
We'll ſet the faſhions too, to half the town;
And then at auctions—money ne'er regard,
Buy pictures like the great, ten pounds a yard;
Zounds, we ſhall make theſe London gentry ſay,
We know what's damn'd genteel as well as they.

FINIS.

www.ingramcontent.com/pod-product-compliance
Lightning Source LLC
Chambersburg PA
CBHW060608030726
47498CB00005B/1601
* 9 7 8 3 3 3 7 0 9 4 7 2 0 *